THE USBORNE

FAIRY TALE TREASURY

The Usborne
Fairy Tale Treasury

Rosie Dickins

Illustrated by Alan Marks

Contents

The Frog Prince

Once upon a time, when magic was much more common than it is today, there was a King who had seven daughters. The six older princesses were all very beautiful but the seventh was so beautiful the sun itself could not outshine her, and her name was Aurora.

One by one, the older princesses got married and left home, until only Aurora was left. She, however, refused to marry.

"Not until I find the perfect prince," she insisted.

One day, Aurora was by herself in the palace gardens. She was playing with a golden ball, throwing it up in the air and catching it again, and laughing merrily. But then she dropped the ball, and it rolled away into a pond and sank into the gloomy depths.

"Oh no," cried Aurora, racing after it. She peered into the dark water, but there was not so much as a gleam of gold.

"How will I get it back?"

"Don't worry," croaked a bright, emerald-green frog, sitting on a lily pad. "I will help you, if you help me in return."

"What do you want?" she asked. "I'll give you my pearl necklace or my golden ring."

"No," said the frog. "I don't want riches. I just want to come home with you, to eat from your own little plate, drink from your own little cup and sleep on your own little pillow."

Aurora looked at the frog's wet, green skin and big, bulgy eyes, and shivered. "Still, he's only a frog," she thought. "He couldn't hop all the way to the palace." So she agreed.

The frog dived deep under the water. When he reappeared, he held a shining golden ball.

"Thank you," cried Aurora. She snatched the ball and set off for the palace at a run.

"Hey, what about your promise?" called the frog, hopping splashily after her. But Aurora pretended not to hear, and he was soon left far behind.

When she got back, Aurora didn't tell anyone about the frog.

In fact, by dinner time she had forgotten all about him. Her six older sisters were visiting and she was busy finding out their news. They were sitting down to eat, chatting happily, when they heard a strange noise.

Hoppity-splash,

hoppity-splash,

hoppity-splash.

Something with wet, webby feet was hopping up the marble staircase.

Aurora's heart sank. "Oh no."

"Princess, youngest Princess, let me in!" came a croak.

"Aurora, open the door," ordered the King.

Hoppity-splash!

A bright, emerald-green frog leaped into the room.

"Who's *that*?" asked the oldest Princess.

"Er, just a frog," replied Aurora. "He helped to get my ball out of the pond and now he wants to come for dinner."

"A frog?" squealed her sisters. "Yuck! Send him away."

"Princess, youngest Princess, have you forgotten your promise?" cried the frog quickly.

"What promise?" asked the King.

The frog fixed Aurora with his big eyes. "To let me eat from your own little plate, drink from your own little cup and sleep on your own little pillow," he said.

"Ugh," said her sisters, shuddering. "Don't let him."

The King looked stern. "Princesses must keep their promises."

So Aurora pressed her lips together, scooped up the frog and carried him to the table. Hoppity-splat! The frog jumped onto her plate. Hoppity-splosh! He dived into her cup.

"Mmm, delicious," he croaked. "Princess, why aren't you eating anything?"

Aurora closed her eyes. "Somehow, I'm not hungry any more," she said faintly.

At last, the meal was over. Aurora couldn't wait to get away. But as soon as she pushed back her chair, the frog called out again. "Princess, youngest Princess, have you forgotten your promise?"

"Princesses must..." began the King.

"...keep their promises, yes, yes I know," muttered Aurora. Her sisters looked on, horrified, as she seized the frog and marched off to her bedroom.

"Awful amphibian," she sighed, dropping him onto her pillow. "I can't believe you're making me do this."

To her surprise, the frog hung his head.

"I'm sorry," he said sadly. "You must find me revolting."

He looked so upset, Aurora found herself feeling sorry

for him. "I don't think you're revolting," she said more kindly. "I'm just not used to frogs."

"But you're so beautiful, and I'm so green and ugly," sniffed the frog. Aurora wanted to cheer him up.

"You're not ugly," she said brightly. "Just, um... perfectly froggy."

And to prove it, she gave him a kiss.

There was a bang and a puff of emerald-green smoke. When the smoke cleared, the frog was gone and a young Prince was standing in his place. Aurora gasped. He was tall and dark and handsome, with bright, emerald-green eyes – and Aurora thought he looked quite perfect.

"Thank you!" cried the Prince. "A wicked witch turned me into a frog, but now you've broken her spell. I'm myself again – and all because of you!" He danced for joy, spinning Aurora around with him.

Aurora blushed. "But I was mean to you," she said.

"Yes, but you were kind too," pointed out the Prince.

"And that's what broke the spell.

Now we can get married and live happily ever after...

that is, if you'd like to marry me?" he added anxiously.

"Oh yes," said Aurora, smiling. "I've been waiting

for my perfect prince. Who'd have thought I'd have

to kiss a frog to find you!"

The Magician's Horse

It was the first day of spring and, all across Persia, people were celebrating. They danced and laughed and picnicked in the warm sunshine. And, beneath the golden domes of his palace, the Sultan was greeting his people.

Among the crowd were many inventors and wise men. The Sultan loved learning, and it was his custom to reward anyone who brought him a new invention.

The palace steps were piled with curious clocks and intriguing astronomical instruments, when a man appeared leading a horse. He pushed his way rudely to the front.

The man had a crooked body and cold eyes, but the horse was magnificent. It had a glossy, ebony-black coat and its saddle sparkled with jewels. But there was something strange about it... It stepped stiffly, without looking left or right.

"Just like clockwork," said Prince Kamar, the Sultan's son. "It's not a real horse – look, it's carved out of wood!"

The man addressed the Sultan. "Your majesty has seen many wonders," he began. "But I promise you have never seen anything as wonderful as my horse."

The Sultan examined the animal. "I see only a moving statue," he observed. "Very lifelike, it's true – but surely any sculptor might do as much."

"I am not a sculptor, I am a magician! And my horse is no statue. I have only to wish myself somewhere, anywhere, and in a few moments I am there. Allow me to show you..."

The Sultan nodded, curious. "There," he said, pointing at a distant peak surrounded by trees. "Bring me a leaf from a tree at the foot of that mountain."

The magician sat in the saddle and touched the horse's side, where a tiny lever was hidden. At once, it tossed its head and sprang into the air. It flashed overhead and vanished into the distance. Moments later, it reappeared over the palace and landed softly. The magician presented a leaf to the Sultan.

"Astonishing!" cried the Sultan. "I've never seen anything like it. This horse will be the pride of my treasure house. Name your reward. What shall it be – gold? Jewels?"

"No, sire. I only desire one thing – to become a prince."

Prince Kamar broke out laughing. "Don't be ridiculous."

The magician glared at the Prince and folded his arms stubbornly. The Sultan hesitated.

"Let me try the horse before you decide anything," suggested Kamar. "After all, it may not work for anyone else."

The Sultan nodded. So Kamar mounted the magnificent steed, and the magician showed him how to take off – but deliberately said nothing about landing. "If he disappears, I can inherit his title," he thought, with a greedy smile.

As soon as Kamar touched the lever, the horse leaped into the air, soaring higher and higher until it was lost from sight. Everyone waited expectantly for his return. Minutes passed, more minutes, an hour... until it began to grow dark.

The Sultan turned to the magician. "What have you done with my son?"

The magician shrugged. "He was too impatient, he took off before I could explain how to land."

The Sultan frowned. "He had better come back safely. Your life shall depend on it! Guards, lock this man up until my son returns."

For his part, Kamar was greatly enjoying his ride. He watched, amazed, as the land unfolded below, with its craggy mountains, green plains, and rivers like rippling silver ribbons, and beyond them strange towns and cities...

Eventually, as the sun began to sink, he decided it was time to go home. He pressed the lever again – but the horse only rose higher. With a jolt, he realized he didn't know how to land.

"I'll just have to work it out," he told himself.

Calmly, he examined the horse. Running his fingers over the polished ebony, he found a second lever on the far side. As soon as he touched it, the horse began to descend, coming to rest on a high marble balcony. By now, the sky was an inky dark, pierced only by twinkling stars.

"Where am I?" wondered the Prince, jumping down.

He peered in at the nearest window and saw a chamber filled with lilies and lotus flowers, and lit by delicately scented candles. In the middle, on silken cushions, sat the most beautiful lady he had ever seen. She had long, dark hair and warm, dark eyes, which blinked in amazement to see Kamar.

"I must be dreaming!" she exclaimed.

"I assure you, lady, I am no dream," Kamar replied. "Although my story is just as strange..." And he told her how he had been carried away by the magician's horse. "Yesterday I was the Prince of Persia. Now I find myself in strange lands, perhaps in danger, at the mercy of a beautiful stranger."

"You are in my lands," the lady replied. "And you are in no danger. I am the Princess Shama. My maids will bring you food and show you where you may sleep."

The Prince nodded gratefully.

Kamar and the Princess spent all of the next day together, and the next, and the next... neither of them had ever met someone whose company delighted them so much.

On the fourth day, the Prince asked the Princess to marry him. "Nothing would make me happier," she said, smiling.

But his next words made her face fall.

"Now I must leave you," he went on. "My father will be worried and I must let him know I am safe. But I will return here as soon as I can, for I cannot be happy without you. Indeed, were it not such a fearful journey, I would take you with me..."

"I'm not afraid of flying," insisted the Princess.

So when Kamar mounted the ebony horse again, the Princess was right behind him. A touch of the lever and it soared obediently into the sky. Even with two riders, it flew just as swiftly as before, and Kamar soon saw the familiar domes of his father's palace.

The Sultan greeted them with delight. As the days had passed, he had begun to fear he would never see his son again. He was thrilled to have Kamar safely back, and to meet his beautiful bride. After hearing their story, the Sultan gave orders to prepare the wedding celebrations at once.

"Oh, and release the magician, too," he added.

The magician was furious about his time in prison. "How dare they lock me up?" he thought bitterly, choosing to forget how he had plotted against the Prince. "It's all Kamar's fault, flying away with my horse like that. And now he comes back with a bride! Well, we'll see about that..."

But he was cunning enough to hide his spite. "A wedding," he said aloud. "How wonderful! The princess should ride to the ceremony on the ebony horse. And this time I will guide it myself, to ensure there are no mishaps."

The hour arrived and the Princess trustingly mounted the horse with the magician. At his touch, the horse hurtled up...

"Slow down," gasped the Princess. But the magician only laughed and flew faster – right past the waiting Prince.

"Come back!" called Kamar. But the wind whipped his words away.

Eventually, the horse landed in a distant forest. The Princess gripped the magician's arm. "Take me back at once!"

"No," he said. "You'll never see your Prince again."

"Help! Please, someone help me!" she shouted.

"Scream all you like," he sneered. "There's no one to hear you." But he was wrong.

"What's going on?" demanded a huge man dressed in furs, pushing his way through the undergrowth. It was a bandit chief named Haman, out hunting from his castle.

"My wife and I were just having an argument," lied the magician quickly.

"That's not true," cried the Princess. "This man is not my husband! I am a Princess and he kidnapped me."

Looking into her beautiful eyes, Haman had no doubt what to do. "Seize this scoundrel!" he told his bandits.

As for the Princess, he bowed and invited her to his castle, and she accepted – little realizing that Haman had no plans to let her go again.

At the castle, the Princess ate and slept, and woke refreshed, to hear the servants chattering about a wedding.

"Who is getting married?" she asked curiously.

"Why, you are!" came the reply. "Lucky you, marrying the chief himself."

She bit her lip. "How can I get out of this?" she wondered.

All of a sudden, she fell to the ground.

"She's fainted with delight," cried a servant, running over.

The Princess opened her eyes and began babbling.

"No, she's delirious," said another. "Fetch the doctors!"

But the doctors couldn't help – and little wonder, since she was only pretending to be ill to avoid Haman. In despair, he ordered his servants to look after her, and offered to reward anyone who could bring about a cure.

Meanwhile, Prince Kamar had set off in search of his beloved. Everywhere he went, he asked the same question: "Have you seen a Princess, a magician and an ebony horse?"

Most people laughed and shook their heads. But eventually, one man paused. "I was passing a bandit's castle when I heard a curious story," he told Kamar. "They say the bandit chief, Haman, rescued a Princess from a magician with an ebony horse. She was so beautiful, Haman was determined to marry her, but she fell into madness before they could hold the ceremony. Now he has offered to reward anyone who cures her."

"But it's no good, she's completely crazy."

"Shama!" thought the Prince, fired with hope. "It must be." And he asked the way to the castle.

A few days later, a man dressed like a doctor knocked at the castle. "I've come to cure the Princess," he said.

He was shown in to the Princess – who immediately pretended to faint. But he whispered something in her ear and, just as suddenly, she sat up and smiled.

"Amazing," cried the bandits. "He must be a great doctor."

"Now leave us," said Kamar (for it was he). "I must finish examining the lady in private."

As soon as they were alone, the young couple worked out a plan... First, the 'doctor' went to see Haman. "To cure the Princess fully, I must know a little more about her history and how she came to your lands," he said.

"She arrived here on a magical horse," said Haman glumly. "Why do you ask?"

"Aha! That's the cause of her madness. The horse's magic has passed into her and made her sick. But I can cure her, if you bring me the horse and the Princess together tomorrow."

Eagerly, Haman agreed.

The next morning, the bandits
brought out the horse and Haman himself
helped the Princess into the saddle.

Then they all stood back and watched as the 'doctor'
lit a bonfire of herbs, chanting strangely.

Thick, scented smoke curled upwards, hiding the horse
from view. It was the moment Kamar had been waiting for.
He leaped onto the horse behind Shama and pressed the lever.

"If a Princess seeks your protection," he called, as they
soared into the sky, "you shouldn't force her to marry you!"

"That's no doctor," Haman yelled. "Seize them!"

But it was too late. The horse had flown away.

So Kamar and Shama returned to Persia and were married,
to great rejoicing – and the magical ebony horse was given pride
of place in the Sultan's treasure house.

As for the magician and the bandit chief,
they were left with nothing but disappointment,
which is all that they deserved.

SLEEPING BEAUTY

There was once a King who lived with his Queen in a fairytale castle overlooking a sparkling lake. They ruled wisely and lacked for nothing, or almost nothing – for although they both loved children, they had never had a child of their own.

Year after year passed, and still they had no child... until one day, as the Queen was walking by the lake, a frog hopped out in front of her. To her astonishment, it bowed and croaked: "Before the year is out, your Majesty, you shall have a daughter."

True to the frog's word, the Queen gave birth to a beautiful baby girl.

"She's as lovely as a rose," sighed the King happily.

"Let's name her Briar-Rose."

To celebrate, the King and Queen gave a great feast.

All the lords and ladies in the kingdom were invited, and all the good fairies. The tables gleamed with real gold plates, and great bunches and garlands of roses filled the air with a sweet scent. Rose lay in her cradle, gurgling happily, while music and laughter echoed around her.

As the good fairies arrived, they waved their wands over the cradle, each giving Rose a magical gift.

"Her beauty will never fade," said Amaryllis, the first fairy.

"And she'll have the wisdom of an angel," added Bluebell, the second.

"She will be graceful in all she does," said Celandine, with an elegant flourish of her wand.

"And dance like a fairy," added Tansy, with a twirl.

"She will sing like a nightingale, and play music to perfection," chorused Snowdrop and Jasmine.

But before Marigold, the last good fairy, could speak, there was a thunderclap and a hunched figure appeared in a cloud of choking purple smoke. It was the bad fairy Nightshade.

"Where was my invitation?" she snarled. "I don't like being left out! I too have a gift for the Princess. On her sixteenth birthday, Briar-Rose will prick her finger on a spinning wheel and die."

The King and Queen gasped. Nightshade cackled and disappeared in another cloud of smoke.

Now, Marigold stepped forward. "I can't undo that curse completely," she said quietly. "Nightshade's magic is too strong. But I can soften it. On her sixteenth birthday, Briar-Rose will prick her finger, but she will not die, only fall into a deep sleep."

"For how long?" whispered the Queen.

"One hundred years," replied the fairy. "Until a prince comes to wake her."

"No," cried the King. "There must be another way. I'll ban spinning! Then she can't prick her finger and the curse can't happen."

Marigold shook her head sadly. "Magic is powerful," she sighed.

Nevertheless, the King did his best. On his orders, all the spinning wheels in the kingdom were broken up and burned. Rose grew up not even knowing such things existed.

Rose was just as beautiful, wise and graceful, and as good at dancing, singing and music, as the fairies had promised. Everyone who saw her loved her, and the King and Queen were very proud. But, as her sixteenth birthday approached, they grew more and more anxious. Finally, the day came – and the palace was again filled with the hustle and bustle of a great celebration.

Guests thronged the rooms, talking and dancing...
Rose's little dog, Bramble, wasn't used to such crowds.
He backed away and ran off to hide.

"Come back!" called Rose. She chased after the dog, up a
winding staircase to the top of a tower. Purple smoke curled out
from under a door, seeming to beckon her inside. Bramble growled.

Curious, Rose pushed open the door, revealing a small round
room lit by a smoky fire. In front of the grate, an old woman
was hunched over a wooden wheel. As the wheel turned, it was
spinning a rough clump of wool into fine, shining thread.
Rose didn't know it, but it was a spinning wheel.

Rose watched curiously. The wheel glimmered in the firelight.
"May I try?" she asked, after a minute.

"Of course, my dear," said the woman.

So Rose took the wheel. "Ow!" she exclaimed. A red stain
bloomed on her fingertip. Then she yawned.

"Excuse me," she sighed, sinking onto a couch. "I'm very
tired all of a sudden." Bramble curled up in her arms and,
a moment later, they were both fast asleep.

The old woman cackled and disappeared in a cloud of
choking purple smoke.

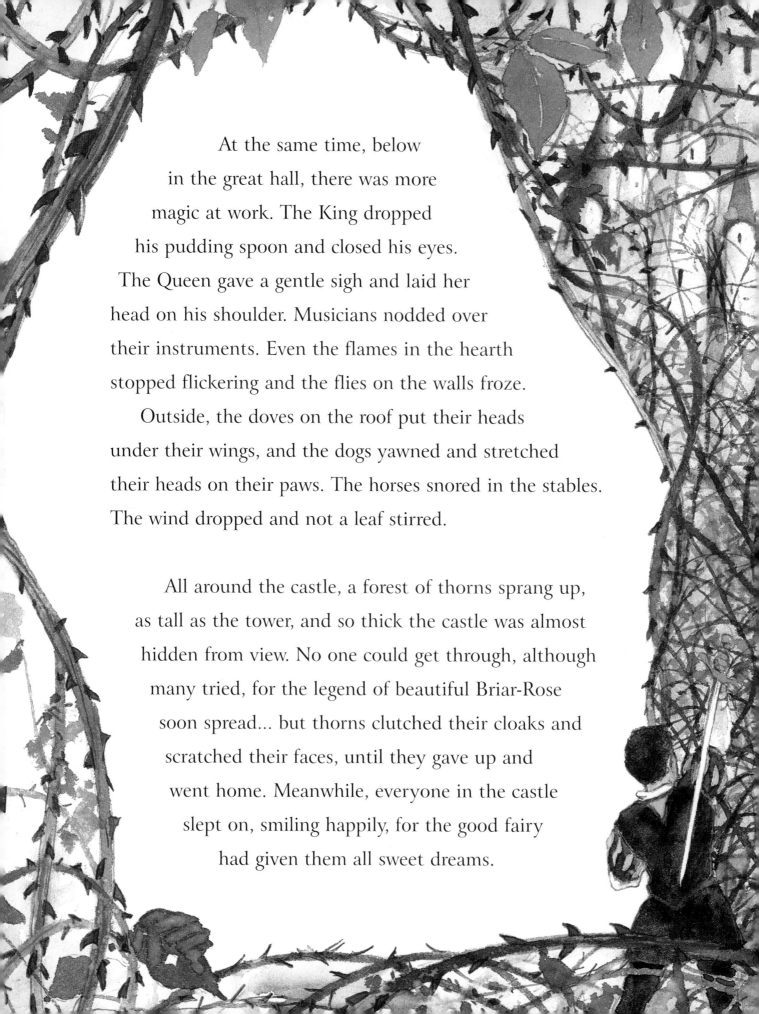

At the same time, below
in the great hall, there was more
magic at work. The King dropped
his pudding spoon and closed his eyes.
The Queen gave a gentle sigh and laid her
head on his shoulder. Musicians nodded over
their instruments. Even the flames in the hearth
stopped flickering and the flies on the walls froze.

Outside, the doves on the roof put their heads
under their wings, and the dogs yawned and stretched
their heads on their paws. The horses snored in the stables.
The wind dropped and not a leaf stirred.

All around the castle, a forest of thorns sprang up,
as tall as the tower, and so thick the castle was almost
hidden from view. No one could get through, although
many tried, for the legend of beautiful Briar-Rose
soon spread... but thorns clutched their cloaks and
scratched their faces, until they gave up and
went home. Meanwhile, everyone in the castle
slept on, smiling happily, for the good fairy
had given them all sweet dreams.

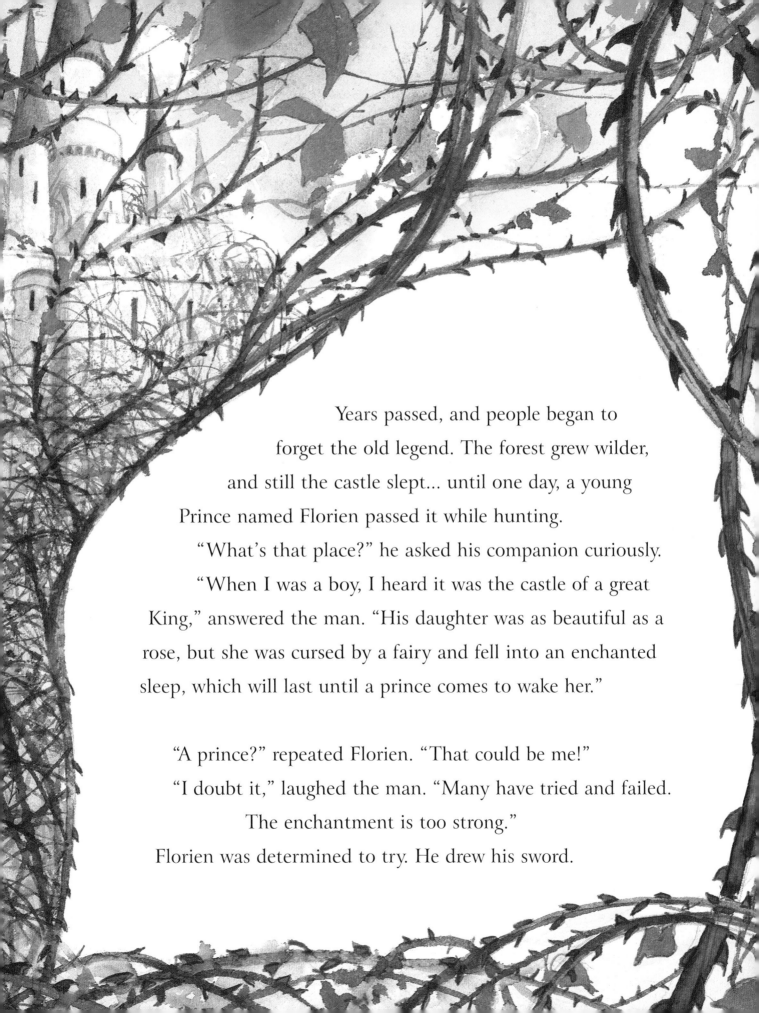

Years passed, and people began to forget the old legend. The forest grew wilder, and still the castle slept... until one day, a young Prince named Florien passed it while hunting.

"What's that place?" he asked his companion curiously.

"When I was a boy, I heard it was the castle of a great King," answered the man. "His daughter was as beautiful as a rose, but she was cursed by a fairy and fell into an enchanted sleep, which will last until a prince comes to wake her."

"A prince?" repeated Florien. "That could be me!"

"I doubt it," laughed the man. "Many have tried and failed. The enchantment is too strong."

Florien was determined to try. He drew his sword.

As soon as his blade touched the wood, the thorns parted of their own accord and burst into bloom.

Florien walked through a tunnel of roses, into a courtyard full of snoring grooms and dogs and horses. He climbed over slumbering guards and entered the castle, where he saw a great hall laid out for a feast. Everywhere, everyone was sound asleep.

The scent of roses drew him on. He climbed a spiral staircase, higher and higher, to a door at the top of a tower.

Inside, asleep on a couch, was the most beautiful Princess he had ever seen.

"She's as lovely as a rose," sighed Florien, falling utterly in love. And, on impulse, he leaned down and kissed her.

Her eyes fluttered open and she smiled. "My Prince," she said. "I saw you in my dreams. I've been waiting for you."

Florien blushed. "My Princess," he replied, taking her hand. "That is, if you will be mine?"

"Oh yes," said Rose, jumping up to lead him downstairs. Bramble followed, wagging his tail merrily.

As Rose got up from the couch on which she had slept away a hundred years, the rest of the castle began to wake up too. Flames flickered and music rang out across the hall. Outside, horses stamped, dogs barked and a fresh breeze – the first for a hundred years – stirred the air.

The King yawned and the Queen looked around in puzzlement. "Where is Briar-Rose?" she wondered, rubbing the sleep from her eyes.

She turned and there was Rose, running down the steps from the turret with her Prince. "Mother, father," she said breathlessly. "Meet Prince Florien – he asked me to marry him, and I said yes!"

"Congratulations!" exclaimed the King and Queen.

Florien and Rose gazed at each other in delight.

"Now this happy ending was worth the wait," came a voice behind them. It was Marigold. Smiling, she waved her wand and the birthday feast became a wedding party – and the celebrations went on all night long, for after a hundred years, no one needed any more sleep.

THE BLUEBIRD

Long ago, in Spain, lived a boy named Bartolo. He had no mother and no father, and he earned a living by making birdcages – big cages, small cages, tall cages and fancy cages – but he was lucky if he sold one a week. So although he worked hard, he rarely had any money or enough to eat.

This morning, Bartolo had woken up starving. "I hope I sell something soon," he thought, as he made his way to the market. A band of musicians was playing merry music to celebrate the Princess's birthday, but his tummy was rumbling so loudly, he hardly noticed.

Crowds came and went, but no one looked at his cages. "Fine birdcages for sale," he called.

A passer-by shrugged. "Who wants to keep caged birds?" he said. "I'd rather see them flying free."

Then Bartolo spotted a stranger with a long velvet cloak – and, perched on his arm, a bird with shining, sky-blue feathers. Bartolo felt a rush of hope.

"Please, sir, will you buy a cage?" he begged.

The stranger shook his head. "I don't need one," he said. "My bird is happy on my arm, as you see."

Bartolo couldn't help it. A tear rolled down his cheek.

"Why, what's the matter?" asked the stranger kindly.

And it all came rushing out – how Bartolo had no money, no food and no customers. "I work and work, but what's the use if I can't sell what I make?" he finished sadly.

The stranger smiled. "I think I can help," he said. He puffed up his cheeks and whistled.

A bright speck appeared in the sky.

It grew bigger and bigger until, with a whirr of wings,

a bird with dazzling, sky-blue feathers landed on

Bartolo's arm. Bartolo cried out in delight.

"This is no ordinary bird," the stranger told him.

"It has magical powers. Just make a wish and say:

Bluest of bluebirds, help me now, and your wish will come true."

"Thank you," gasped Bartolo, stroking the bird's sleek blue

feathers. When he looked up, the stranger had vanished.

Bartolo knew immediately what to wish for. Breakfast!

"Bluest of bluebirds, help me now," he whispered – and a plate

of hot, sweet rolls and a steaming mug of chocolate appeared

in front of him. "Amazing! That's magic."

He broke open a roll and offered some to the bird.

Then he ate... and ate...

until he could eat no more.

In the distance, something caught his eye. He squinted into the sun. A crowd of grandly dressed lords and ladies were arriving at the castle on the hill.

"Of course, it's the Princess's birthday," Bartolo remembered. "She'll be having a wonderful party. I'd love to go. I wonder..."

He looked down at his rags. "Bluest of bluebirds, help me now." In the blink of an eye, he was wearing a fine velvet suit. "Now I look just like a lord!" he cried. And he set off for the castle with the bird on his arm.

Inside the castle, however, things were not going to plan. There was to have been a great feast, with music and dancing – but the cook had burned the cakes and bungled the buns, and the court musicians had all caught colds and were sneezing too much to play.

The poor Princess was nearly in tears when Bartolo arrived. He saw instantly what was wrong.

"I think I can help," he said, bowing low to the Princess.

"If you will allow me?"

"Oh yes, please!" she said at once, jumping as several musicians blew their noses loudly behind her.

Bartolo looked around and wished. "Bluest of bluebirds, help me now."

Suddenly, the tables were loaded with delicious cakes and glorious sticky buns, and the musicians stopped sneezing and struck up a waltz...

He turned back to the Princess. "May I have this dance?" he asked, and the Princess nodded gratefully.

As they whirled across the ballroom, Bartolo called on the bluebird again and again, conjuring up gifts for the Princess – bracelets of rubies, pearl rings and strings of sapphires...

"Happy Birthday," he whispered, with a smile that made the Princess blush with happiness.

"This is the best birthday ever," she sighed.

The King was watching closely. "That bird has magical powers," he realized. "Just think how rich it could make me. I've got to have it!" So, when the dance was over, he summoned Bartolo. "How much do you want for that bird?" he asked.

"It's not for sale," replied Bartolo firmly.

"I'll give you a chest full of gold?" offered the King.

"No," said Bartolo.

"My castle?" said the King.

"No," said Bartolo. "There's only one thing I want."

"What's that?" the King asked curiously.

"Your daughter's hand in marriage," replied Bartolo. "That is, if she will have me."

The Princess smiled at Bartolo. "I will," she said.

"Very well," agreed the King hastily.

So Bartolo made one last wish. "Bluest of bluebirds, help me now," he whispered, and a golden carriage drew up at the door, to carry him and his bride to their new home – a gleaming palace that had just appeared on the horizon.

Then he gently handed the bird to the King, helped the Princess into the carriage and drove off.

"This bird will make me the wealthiest man in the world," chuckled the King, as he watched them go.

"But sire," said the chief musician suddenly. "Are you sure that's the right bird?"

The King glanced down – and his jaw dropped. The precious bluebird had turned into a raggedy old crow. It fixed him with a beady eye, cawed loudly and flapped away.

The birthday guests burst out laughing. "That's what you get for being so greedy," they said.

And what about Bartolo and his princess bride? They lived happily together for the rest of their days, and Bartolo never went hungry again.

THE YOUNGEST PRINCESS

Once upon a time, there was a King with three daughters. He loved them all dearly, and was loved by them in return. But as the King grew old, he grew distrustful, and longed to test their love. So one day, he summoned them before him.

"My daughters," he said. "How much do you love me?"

"As much as light and life," answered the first Princess.

"Better than all the world," said the second Princess.

The King nodded and smiled, well-pleased. The youngest Princess, Grizelda, stood shy and thoughtful.

"Well?" he prompted.

"I love you as much as salt," she said at last.

The King frowned. "As much as salt?" he repeated disbelievingly.

"Salt is cheap and common!" he snapped. "You speak as if you are the daughter of a cook, not a King. Speak again."

But Grizelda's eyes shimmered with unshed tears, and she could not speak for the lump in her throat.

Her silence enraged the King. "To love your royal father no better than salt!" he cried. "Ungrateful child. You are no daughter of mine. Get out!"

Weeping, Grizelda ran out of the castle. She ran until she could run no more, and then she walked. Eventually, as the sun was setting, she came to an inn. By now, she was very tired and she had nowhere else to go, so she knocked at the door.

"Please, can you give me a job?" she begged.

The innkeeper glanced curiously at her muddy silk dress and delicate hands. "What kind of job?" he asked. "You don't look as if you're used to working."

"No, but I'll work hard and I'm willing to learn," promised Grizelda in reply.

The innkeeper looked into her open, honest face. "Why, she's only a girl," he realized. "Come in," he said kindly. "As it happens, I could use someone to help with the cooking."

True to her word, Grizelda worked hard and learned fast. Soon, people were visiting the inn from far and wide to taste her food – from rich soups and spicy stews to crackling roasts and creamy puddings.

And so the inn flourished, and the fame of its cook spread, until news reached the castle, where Grizelda's sisters were planning the King's birthday.

"Let's send for this cook," suggested the eldest Princess. "Some good food might cheer everyone up. It's been so sad ever since Grizelda went."

Her sister nodded. It was true. Everyone was missing the youngest Princess badly, especially the King. As soon as his temper had cooled, he had sent messengers with his apologies to bring her home again. But no one had been able to find her, for no one dreamed she might be working in the kitchen of a country inn.

So imagine the sisters' joy and amazement when the cook they had sent for finally arrived. "Grizelda," they cried, flinging their arms around her. "Oh, how we've missed you."

"I missed you too," she said softly, hugging them back. "Now listen, I have a plan..."

The King's birthday dawned bright and sunny. The great hall of the castle was decorated with streamers and garlands, and servants dashed to and fro, setting the tables. In the kitchens, Grizelda was cooking up a feast fit for a king.

She had planned the menu with care. There were to be a dozen courses of a dozen dishes each, followed by an enormous birthday cake covered in silver stars and golden crowns.

A fanfare sounded and the guests began to arrive. As they sat down to eat, the hall filled with appreciative sighs and murmurs. But the King ignored them all and sat in silence, brooding miserably about Grizelda.

"You must eat, Father," said the eldest Princess gently.

With a sigh, the King lifted his fork… "Ugh," he exclaimed. "What's wrong with this food? It has no taste."

The middle Princess caught her sister's eye and smiled. "Perhaps you'd prefer some soup," she suggested, handing him a heavy silver bowl.

The King tried a spoonful – and stared at his bowl in disgust. "This is awful," he moaned. "I can't taste a thing. Bring me something else!"

A servant came running with a silver tureen brimming with steaming-hot stew. The King usually loved stew. But this time, he took a cautious taste and dropped his spoon with a clatter.

"Pass the salt," he snapped.

But strange to say, there was no salt on the table.

The King had had enough. "Bring me the cook!"

The cook appeared, wiping her hands on her apron, and curtseyed to the King.

"What are you playing at?" the King demanded. "None of this food has any taste! You left out the salt."

"Forgive me, your Majesty," said the cook. "But I didn't dare to add any salt. You banished your daughter because she said she loved you as much as salt; you told her salt was cheap and common. So I thought you must prefer your food without it."

The cook's voice was strangely familiar. The King peered at the face beneath the large cook's hat.

"Grizelda," he cried, jumping up to embrace her. "Oh, how I've missed you. Now I understand what you were trying to tell me. I was foolish, and you were wiser than I knew. We cannot live without salt! Without it, nothing has any taste."

So the King and his daughters were reunited at last, and sat down to eat together. After the King had sprinkled his food with salt, it tasted better than anything he had ever eaten. And with each bite, he grew still happier, as he realized how precious was a love like salt.

Prince Ivan
and the Firebird

The Tsar of Russia was very proud of his garden, which was full of rare trees that grew nowhere else in the world. Some of the trees bore beautifully scented flowers, others were laden with heavy, jewel-like fruits. Most precious of all was an ancient apple tree, whose rustling leaves sheltered fruit of solid gold.

The Tsar treasured this tree, and visited it every day. To his dismay, one morning he noticed an apple was missing.

"A thief must have sneaked in during the night!" he cried, ordering extra guards all around the garden.

But it was no good. The next day, another apple had mysteriously disappeared.

"I'll catch the thief," promised the Tsar's eldest son, Prince Dimitri. That night, Dimitri went and sat right under the tree... but by midnight, he was fast asleep and, in the morning, another apple had gone.

"Dimitri must have dozed off," said the Tsar's second son, Prince Vasili. "*I'll* catch the thief." So that night, he went and sat under the tree... but by midnight, he too had fallen fast asleep.

In the morning, yet another apple had vanished.

The Tsar was furious.

"Father, please let me try to catch the thief," begged his youngest son, Prince Ivan.

"How will you succeed, when your brothers have failed?" grumbled the Tsar.

But Ivan insisted and, at nightfall, went to sit under the tree. It grew darker and darker. Slowly, he felt his eyes begin to close and pinched himself to stay awake.

Just after midnight, the garden was lit with a flickering golden light. Ivan looked up – and gasped. Soaring over the wall was a bird with flaming, red-gold feathers. It shone so brightly, it made night seem like day.

Dazzled, Ivan watched the bird
land on the tree and pluck an apple in its beak.
Then he leaped up and grabbed its tail. "Got you!" But the
bird flapped and fluttered, and pulled itself free – leaving Ivan
grasping one fiery golden tail feather.

In the morning, Ivan showed his father the feather, still flickering with golden fire. Dimitri and Vasili looked on jealously as he told his father about the strange bird.

"Amazing," muttered the Tsar. "I must see this myself." He sat up all the next night, and the next... but the Firebird did not come back.

"Little brother must have scared it away," said Dimitri scornfully. "I will bring it back." He took the finest horse from the stable and set out. But days passed and he did not return.

"I will go after him," said Vasili. "I am sure *I* can find the bird." He took a second horse and set out. But more days passed and Vasili did not return either.

"Let me go after them," pleaded Ivan, ignoring the Tsar's frowns. "I'll bring back the Firebird!"

"How will you succeed, when your brothers haven't even returned?" sighed the Tsar. But Ivan insisted and, in the end, his father had to let him go. "But I can't spare another horse!" he said grumpily. So Ivan set off on foot.

Ivan was striding through a forest when he heard an animal howling. He searched around, and found a huge, shaggy wolf caught in a trap.

"Poor thing," said Ivan, setting it free at once.

"Thank you," growled the wolf. "You are the third person to come down this road, but the first to help me. Now I will serve you in return."

"A talking wolf!" exclaimed Ivan. "Well, one magical animal might know another. Can you help me to find the Firebird?"

The wolf nodded a shaggy head. "Climb on my back and I will take you to it," it replied.

So Ivan scrambled up, holding tightly to the wolf's thick coat, and they set off. The wolf ran faster than the wind, forests and fields flying by. Ivan had never journeyed so quickly.

They had soon left Russia far behind.

Eventually, the wolf stopped by a stone birdhouse.

"You will find the Firebird in there, in a golden cage," it said. "Take the bird, but leave the cage!"

The inside of the house flickered with the light from the bird's feathers. Everything was just as the wolf described, but Ivan hesitated.

"I should really take the whole cage," he thought. "Or the bird might fly away."

He reached out... but as soon as he lifted the cage, bells began to clang and guards came running. Ivan was captured and dragged before the Queen of the land.

"You were trying to steal my bird," cried the Queen. "I should have you executed! But I've been looking for someone bold to bring me the Fire Horse, with its flaming mane and tail. So I'll let you go – in fact I'll give you the Firebird – if you bring the Fire Horse back for me."

Ivan had no choice but to agree.

"Wolf, what have I done?" he moaned. "I should have listened to you."

"You were foolish," agreed the wolf, with a growl. "But I will help you. Climb on."

Once again, the wolf ran faster than the wind, over hills and mountains, to an even more remote kingdom.

The wolf stopped by a stone stable.

"The Fire Horse is there," it told Ivan. "Take the horse, but don't touch the golden bridle."

Inside the stable was a horse with a blazing, red-gold coat. As it tossed its head, the light from its mane glinted across a golden bridle hanging on the wall.

Again, Ivan hesitated. "How will I lead the horse without its bridle?" he thought, reaching out... but as soon as he touched the straps, bells clanged and grooms came running. They dragged Ivan before their King.

"You were trying to steal my horse," thundered the King. "I should kill you now! But I've been looking for someone bold to bring me the Fire Maiden, with her beautiful golden hair. I intend to marry her."

"So," the King went on, "I'll let you go – in fact I'll give you the horse – if you fetch the Fire Maiden for me."

Again, Ivan could only nod.

"Wolf, I've done it again," he sighed.

"You should have followed my advice," growled the wolf. "But I will help you. Climb on."

Faster than the wind, the wolf carried Ivan almost to the edge of the world. It stopped by a stone palace where a maiden was walking. Ivan had never seen anyone so beautiful. Her soft, golden hair rippled with light, like living flames.

Ivan leaped off the wolf and made a deep bow.

"Who are you?" cried the maiden, startled.

"Forgive my boldness," said Ivan. "I have crossed the world to find you."

The maiden smiled and blushed, and invited Ivan in for tea. She was charmed by how handsome and kind he was – and he was just as charmed with her.

"Wolf," he moaned later. "How can I take the maiden to the King? I'm falling in love with her myself!"

"Do not despair," growled the wolf.

"I have a plan..."

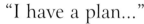

So the wolf carried two figures back to the King, one a handsome young Prince and one a dazzling maiden – but the 'Prince' had lengths of glowing golden hair hidden under a cap, and the 'maiden' was swathed in veils. Ivan and the maiden had changed clothes, and the wolf had added a touch of magic, to prevent the King from seeing through the disguise.

The maiden handed over Ivan, and the King happily gave her the Fire Horse in exchange. Then she rode away, and the King gave orders for the wedding feast to be prepared.

"I'd like to take a walk in the grounds," whispered Ivan through his veils.

"Of course, my sweet," purred the King.

Ivan made straight for the stable, where the others were waiting for him. They pulled off their disguises and rode away, Ivan on the wolf and the maiden on the Fire Horse.

They had not gone far when they heard a yell.

"Hey! Come back."

The King was chasing after them, but the wolf and the Fire Horse ran faster than the wind, and he could not catch them.

"Now for the Queen," said Ivan. "Although it seems a shame to part with this horse."

The wolf grinned. "Perhaps you can keep it, if you do exactly as I say."

When they arrived, the Fire Maiden waited outside while Ivan led in the wolf – but it no longer looked like a wolf. It was brushed and beribboned and, with a magnificent saddle cloth and a touch of magic, appeared just like the Fire Horse. The Queen clapped her hands in delight and gave Ivan the Firebird.

As soon as the Queen left the wolf alone, he tore off the saddle cloth and dashed after his friends. Behind him, the Queen screamed. "Hey! Come back!"

But the wolf and the Fire Horse ran faster than the wind, and the Queen's cries were lost in the distance. Soon, they were back in the forest.

"I will leave you here," the wolf told Ivan. "You are nearly home, but don't stop for anyone until you get there."

So Ivan and the Fire Maiden went on together, but they had not gone far when they bumped into Ivan's brothers. They had long since given up on their quest and had been spending their time hunting instead.

"Little brother," they called and, forgetting the wolf's warning, Ivan stopped. "What have you got there?" they asked.

So Ivan introduced them to the Fire Maiden and told them about his adventures.

The brothers pretended to congratulate him but, as soon as his back was turned, they scowled. "These trophies should be ours," they muttered. And they hatched a terrible plot...

"Have a drink with us," they told Ivan. "To celebrate your success."

"With pleasure, my brothers," said Ivan. But his cup was drugged and he fell into a deep sleep. His brothers tied him to a tree and left him for the wolves to devour, while they rode off with the Firebird, horse and maiden – threatening her with terrible things if she gave them away.

When Ivan woke, he was alone in the dark.

"What shall I do now?" he thought in despair. Then he heard a howl and a familiar, fierce face appeared.

"Wolf!"

"You should have listened to me," growled the wolf. "But I will help you one last time." It bared its teeth and Ivan flinched, but it only gnawed through the ropes. "Now climb on," said the wolf. "We don't have much time."

Faster than the wind, the wolf carried Ivan back to his father's palace. The garden was lit up with lanterns and they could hear the sounds of a great banquet.

"What's going on?" Ivan asked a guard.

"The Tsar is celebrating the return of Princes Dimitri and Vasili," came the reply. "And their treasures – although those aren't so wonderful, if you ask me... a bird that will not sing, a horse that will not eat and a maiden who won't stop weeping!"

Ivan did not wait to hear any more, but rushed into the banqueting hall. Ivan's brothers turned pale, but the Fire Maiden rushed into his arms, smiling and wiping away her tears. The Firebird burst into song, making all the flowers in the garden bloom, and the Fire Horse whinnied for joy.

Then Ivan told the Tsar what had really happened and in fury he banished the treacherous brothers. But Ivan and the maiden were married and lived happily for the rest of their days.

As for the Tsar's garden, the wonderful golden apple tree now had a golden bird living among its branches and a golden horse grazing beneath it... and the only thing Ivan and his bride treasured more was the friendship of a grizzled old wolf.

The Fairy at the Well

There were once two sisters named Alise and Amie, who were as different as night from day. For while Amie worked and worked, and had a sweet smile for everyone, Alise never lifted a finger and always wore a surly frown. In this, Alise was the mirror of her mother. And, as people often prefer their own likeness, so the mother doted on Alise and was quick to find fault with Amie.

One hot summer's day, their mother shouted for Amie to fetch fresh water from the well. "And be quick about it!" she added sharply. Amie picked up a pitcher and hurried off...

69

The path to the well was dusty and dry, and Amie was very thirsty by the time she got there. She hauled up a bucket and emptied it carefully into the pitcher. Then she lifted it, to take a sip of cool, clear water, when she heard a frail voice. She turned and saw an old woman with silvery hair.

"May I have some of your water?" said the woman.

"Gladly," Amie told her. "I am sorry I have no cup, but I will hold my pitcher so you may drink from it." And instead of drinking herself, she offered the water to the woman.

The woman took a long sip. "Thank you, my dear," she said, with a smile. "Your kindness deserves a reward. I see you are as sweet as a rose and as pure as a diamond – so when you speak, roses and diamonds shall fall from your lips."

"Thank you," said Amie. "Oh!" A pink rosebud and two blue diamonds fell to the ground in front of her. She bent to pick them up. When she looked up, the woman had vanished.

Amie seized the pitcher and rushed home in excitement.

"What took you so long?" snapped her mother.

As Amie told her story, a heap of sparkling jewels and soft-as-silk roses piled up in front of her. Her mother's eyes widened.

"...she must have been a fairy!" finished Amie.

Three white roses and as many glittering diamonds joined the heap.

Her mother smiled greedily. "Alise!" she called. "Come in here! Take this pitcher to the well at once. And when an old woman asks for water, make sure you give her some."

"Why can't Amie go?" moaned Alise.

"Just do as I tell you!" shouted her mother.

So Alise set off, dragging her feet. "All this way, just for some old woman," she muttered. She hauled up the bucket in a very bad temper, slopping and spilling plenty. "Stupid water!"

Then, she heard a frail voice. "May I have some water?"

"I don't see why you can't get your own," said Alise, flinging the half-empty pitcher at her.

The woman frowned. "I see you are as mean and lazy as a toad," she said. "So when you speak, toads shall fall from your lips."

"Ha ha, very funny," snapped Alise – and clapped her hands to her mouth. Four ugly, spotted toads had dropped onto the ground in front of her. She left the pitcher and ran home as fast as she could.

"Help!" she croaked. "Look what's happened."

Four fat toads slithered from her lips.

"Ugh – toads!" screamed her mother. She turned on Amie. "This is all your fault. Get out! I never want to see you again."

Amie fled, tears trickling down her cheek. She was so upset that she didn't look where she was going – until she nearly collided with a tall, chestnut horse.

"Whoa!" came a voice. Amie blinked and looked up, to see a handsome Prince on the horse's back. He smiled kindly. "What's the matter?" he asked, offering her a handkerchief.

Amie wiped her eyes and told him, while diamonds and roses fell at her feet.

"But it wasn't your fault at all!" exclaimed the Prince indignantly. His heart went out to the homeless girl. "Why don't you come to the palace with me?"

"Oh, but," began Amie. "I'm just a poor girl..."

"With a fairy gift like yours, no one will call you poor," laughed the Prince, gallantly helping her onto his horse.

So Amie went to live in the palace, where she and the Prince soon fell in love and married. But no one wanted to marry awful Alise. Instead, she and her mother spent the rest of their days snapping and shouting and surrounded by toads.

As for the fairy at the well, she may be there still.

CINDERELLA

Once upon a time, there was a beautiful young girl named Ella. Her mother had died and, after a few years, her father married again, bringing a step-mother and two step-sisters to live with them.

The step-mother had a plain face and a proud nature, and the sight of Ella's golden hair and sweet smile filled her with jealousy. "I must do something about that girl," she decided. "Let's see how pretty she looks doing the housework."

"Scrub the floor!" she snapped spitefully.

"Yes, step-mother," said Ella.

"Stoke the fire and stir the soup."

"Yes, step-mother."

"Scour the dishes and sweep the steps and sew the buttons on the shirts..."

Ella did her best, but as soon as she finished one chore, her step-mother gave her two more...

Eventually, she was so exhausted that she fell asleep beside the kitchen fire. When she woke, she was covered in ashes and cinders.

"Look at you," giggled her step-sisters. "We should call you Cinderella!" Before long, everyone was calling her Cinderella and treating her like a maid, and her father was too afraid of her step-mother to do anything about it.

Now Cinderella had to spend all her time cleaning and cooking, while her step-mother and step-sisters sat around sipping tea and scolding her. Soon, her dresses were worn to rags, though her beauty still outshone everyone around her.

She never cried or complained, and only shared her troubles with one friend – a little white dove which lived in the garden. Each evening, she fed it with crumbs and, when she felt sad, it would perch on her shoulder and coo softly until she smiled again.

One day, while Cinderella was sweeping the hall, a messenger knocked with a royal invitation.

The King and Queen are holding a ball for their son, Prince Charming, at the palace tomorrow night, to help the Prince to choose a bride. All eligible young ladies are invited to attend.

God save the King!

"A ball?" screeched the step-sisters. "With Prince Charming? We'll need new ballgowns. At once, Mama!" And they started arguing about what they would wear and which of them the Prince would dance with first...

"Please," said Cinderella softly. "May I go too?"

"I don't see why not," said her father timidly. "The invitation does say *all* eligible young ladies."

"Cinderella?" laughed his wife. "They wouldn't let in a ragamuffin like her!" She turned to Cinderella. "Stop idling and fetch the dress-maker. Your sisters need new gowns."

"Yes, and bring the shoe-maker too," put in the older sister, tapping her big, clumpy feet. "I need new dancing shoes, for when the Prince dances with me!"

"Don't forget the hairdresser," added the younger sister, tossing her lank, mousy hair. "When the Prince sees my curls, he'll marry me on the spot."

Cinderella spent the next day running to and fro with combs and curling tongs, perfumes and jewels...

She ironed petticoats and tied ribbons, while her step-mother and step-sisters tried on new outfits and admired themselves in huge, floor-length mirrors.

At last their carriage arrived and they swept out, wrapped in velvet cloaks, diamonds glinting in their hair.

"Sorry, dear," whispered Cinderella's father, as he followed them into the night. Then the front door slammed, and Cinderella was alone in the silent house.

A tear splashed onto the floor. "Oh, I wish I was going too," she sighed, rubbing her eyes.

Just then, there was a tap at the door. Cinderella opened it, to reveal an old lady grasping a silvery stick. Cinderella's dove was sitting on her shoulder.

"Wh-who are you?" asked Cinderella, startled.

"Your fairy godmother," the old lady replied.

"My fairy godmother?" repeated Cinderella in bewilderment. "I – I never knew I had one!"

"I'm here to grant your wish – you shall go to the ball! But first, I need a pumpkin."

Cinderella blinked. "A pumpkin?"

But she was too polite to argue, so she led her visitor into the garden and picked the biggest, roundest pumpkin she could find.

The fairy tapped it with her stick. There was a shower of stars and then, instead of a pumpkin, there stood a round, golden carriage. Cinderella gasped.

"Now horses," muttered her godmother, peering around. "Ah, this should do." She tapped a mousehole and, one by one, six mice came trotting out. Tap-tap-tap, and they turned into six fine, dappled horses. Then a rat scurried past – tap – and became a plump coachman with a whiskery beard.

The fairy turned to Cinderella. "There are two lizards under that bush. Could you fetch them?" Tap-tap, and the lizards became footmen in sleek, smooth coats.

"But godmother, what about my dress?" said Cinderella, glancing down at her rags.

"Oh yes, I almost forgot." Tap – a shower of stars, and Cinderella was wearing a beautiful ballgown of blue and silver satin. Dainty glass slippers sparkled on her feet.

Cinderella twirled around in delight, her slippers tinkling on the ground. "Oh thank you, fairy godmother!"

"Make haste now," said the fairy. "And enjoy the ball! But don't forget – my magic will fade at midnight, so you must leave before the clock strikes twelve."

There was a great commotion at the ball when the golden
carriage drew up. No one recognized the lady in the blue
and silver dress, not even her family. "She must be a foreign
Princess," people whispered. "She's so beautiful!"

The Prince came up to her and bowed. "May I have this
dance?" he asked softly.

"Oh yes," said Cinderella, looking into his clear, dark eyes.

All night, the Prince danced with no one but Cinderella.
They whirled and twirled gracefully across the ballroom together,
in time to the music...

Cinderella was so happy, she completely forgot about the time – until a clock began to strike.

"Midnight," she gasped, stopping in the middle of a minuet. She dashed out of the room so fast that one of her slippers slid off. She didn't even pause to pick it up.

"Come back," called the Prince, racing after her. "You haven't told me your name." But, by the time he reached the door, she had vanished. Puzzled, he summoned the palace guards.

"Which way did the Princess go?"

"What Princess?" exclaimed the chief guard.

"No one has come past. No one except a kitchen maid, anyway."

The Prince was baffled, but he refused to give up hope.
"I *will* find my Princess," he said stubbornly.

"And then I'll marry her!"

The following morning, the step-sisters talked of nothing but the ball. Cinderella listened quietly.

"Of course the Prince wanted to dance with me," one was saying. "He was just being polite, dancing with that woman..." She was interrupted by a voice outside.

"Hear ye, hear ye. The Prince wishes to announce he will marry the owner of this glass slipper!"

The step-sisters flung open the door and grabbed the messenger. "It's mine!" they shrieked simultaneously, both trying to seize the slipper at once.

The oldest rammed in a clumpy foot. "Look, a perfect fit," she lied.

"No, your heel is sticking out," snorted the other. But when she tried it on, her toes wouldn't even go in.

The messenger paid them no attention. He was gazing at Cinderella with clear, dark eyes. "Will you try too?" he asked.

"Oh no, she's just the maid," said her step-mother quickly.

The messenger ignored her. He held out the sparkling slipper and Cinderella raised one tiny foot. The slipper slid on like a glove. It was a perfect fit.

"I knew it was you," cried the messenger, throwing off his hat and cloak. "Cinderella, will you marry me?"

"My Prince!" said Cinderella in delight. "Of course I will."

There was a shower of stars, and Cinderella's fairy godmother reappeared, with the dove on her shoulder.

"We've come for the wedding," she said. She tapped her stick, and Cinderella found herself wearing a wedding dress of white and gold, embroidered all over with pearls.

Then the dove fluttered up with a rose. "Thank you," whispered Cinderella, tucking it into the Prince's buttonhole.

So Cinderella and her Prince were married and lived happily ever after – but her step-sisters were not so lucky. With Cinderella gone, their mother made them do all the housework, and she never stopped scolding them for having such big feet.

THE MAGIC TINDERBOX

One cold winter's day, a young soldier named Max came marching over the hills. He had fought bravely in the wars, but now peace had come and he was out of a job – so he was off to seek his fortune.

As he passed a ramshackle cottage, he saw an old woman stooped over a well. She was very old and very ugly. In fact, she was a witch! But Max didn't know that, and he greeted her with a smile. "Good day, Granny," he called.

"Young man," croaked the witch. "My tinderbox has fallen down this well. Can you get it out? I can't light my fire without it."

Max peered into the inky dark.

"This is no ordinary well," went on the witch. "It is full of treasure. If you can rescue my tinderbox, you may take as much as you want!"

"My fortune has found me!" thought Max, happily. "Can you let me down in the bucket?" he asked.

"Yes," croaked the witch. "There's only one problem. The contents of the well are guarded by three giant dogs. The first has eyes as big as saucers, the second has eyes like dinner plates, and the eyes of the third are as huge as mill wheels..."

Brave as he was, Max hesitated.

"...so you will need this," continued the witch. And she handed him a little bag of powder. "Just sprinkle a bit in their eyes and they will fall asleep on the instant."

So Max climbed into the bucket and the witch let him down, creaking and clanking, lower... and lower...

into the damp, dark well.

He braced himself for a splash, but instead the bucket hit solid ground – bump – and he tumbled out onto a pebbly floor.

He was in a huge, shadowy cave. Through the gloom, he could just make out a coppery glow and a pair of watchful, saucer-sized eyes.

"You must be the first dog," said Max. "Aren't you a handsome fellow!" There was no sign of the tinderbox.

The dog started to growl, with a rumble like thunder. Quickly, Max threw a pinch of powder – and it lowered its head and began to snore.

Max scooped up a handful of copper and made his way through the cave. A little further on, mounds of silver gleamed in the dim light, watched by eyes as big as dinner plates.

"Here's the second dog," muttered Max, as it stood up and howled, sending pieces of silver cascading in every direction. "What a voice!" But another pinch of powder and it lay down quietly and went to sleep.

Max picked up a pocketful of silver and went on, until he came to a mountain of glimmering gold – under the unblinking gaze of two gigantic eyes, eyes as huge as mill wheels...

"The third dog," said Max. "It's rude to stare, you know!" In answer, the dog only roared – but so loudly, the floor shook.

Hastily, Max threw the rest of the powder. As soon as the dust touched the dog, it too fell asleep. "Whew! Now, where's that tinder box?"

Max looked around, until he spotted an old metal box between the dog's paws. He tucked it into his pocket. Then, since his pockets were full, he took off his cap and filled it with gold. "I'll never be poor again," he sighed.

Max tiptoed, jingling, past the sleeping dogs and into the bucket. "I've got it," he called. Creaking and clanking, the bucket began to rise. But just below the top, it jerked to a halt.

"A bit further," called Max. "Keep pulling!"

"Pass me the tinderbox first, dearie," said the witch. "Just in case you drop it."

Max clung to the swaying bucket, suddenly suspicious. "Don't worry," he said. "It's safe in my pocket."

"I said, pass it up," snapped the witch. "I want it now!"

"Let me out first," insisted Max. "Or how do I know you won't let me fall?"

"If you won't let me have it, then I WILL let you fall," screeched the witch, letting go of the rope. The bucket hurtled down and hit the bottom – BANG!

"And there you can stay, you useless good-for-nothing," she shouted. A cover thudded over the top of the well and everything went dark.

Max shook the dust off himself. It was so dark he could barely see. "Let me out!" he cried. But no one answered.

"This is a pretty pickle I'm in," he thought ruefully. "All this gold and I can't even buy myself dinner or a chair by the fire… fire… the tinderbox!"

He pulled it out and opened the lid. Inside was a flint, a lump of steel and a candle stub. "I wonder why the old woman wanted this so badly? Still, at least I can have some light."

Max struck the flint against the steel, sending up a shower of hot blue sparks, and lit the candle. As it flared, he glanced around for a way out, but there was none.

"What orders, Master?" came a growl behind him.

Max jumped and turned. Behind him, glowing in the dark, was a pair of eyes – eyes like saucers. Max swallowed hard.

"Do not fear," went on the dog. "Whoever holds the tinderbox is our master. One strike, and I will do your bidding. Two strikes, and the dog who guards the silver will come to you. Three, and the dog who guards the gold is yours to command.

What do you wish?"

"To be well away from here, safe and sound in a nice warm inn," replied Max. "With dinner on the table and a soft feather bed for the night."

No sooner said than done, the dog leaped forward and carried him to an inn. The inn keeper was very surprised to find the soldier there. "I didn't hear you come in," he grumbled. But his eyes lit up when Max pulled out a gold piece. The soldier was quickly settled in the best room, with a fine dinner in front of him.

The next day, Max bought a stylish new suit and a high-stepping horse, and rode out to see the town. He looked very handsome in his finery.

In the distance, a copper castle glinted. "Who lives there?" he asked a passerby.

"The Princess," came the reply. "She's very beautiful, but no one is allowed to see her. The King keeps her locked away because it is said she will marry a common soldier, and he is determined not to let that happen."

Max was very curious about the hidden Princess. The more he thought about her, the more he longed to see her.

"I wonder..." he thought, looking at his tinderbox.

That night, he struck the flint once. Immediately, the dog with eyes like saucers stood before him.

"I want to see the Princess," said Max.

The dog disappeared and, in the blink of a saucer-sized eye, returned with the Princess on its back. She had shining copper hair, and a gown of silver and gold, and was even more beautiful than Max had imagined. She was so beautiful, he couldn't help kissing her – and she gave him a radiant smile before the dog carried her back.

Over breakfast, the Princess told the King about a strange dream. "I thought a dog with eyes like saucers took me to see a handsome soldier," she said. The King frowned.

Max spent all the next day thinking about the Princess. As soon as night fell, he struck the flint twice and the dog with dinner-plate eyes appeared.

"I want to see the Princess," he said.

So the dog brought her, and Max was so delighted to see her, he didn't notice its dusty pawprints. The King had scattered flour all around the copper castle, so that anyone coming or going would leave a trail of prints. Luckily for Max, before the King could follow the trail, a shower of rain washed all the prints away.

Still, the King was determined to find out what was going on. On the third night, he set extra guards around the Princess's room. This time, Max struck the flint three times, for the dog with eyes like mill wheels.

The dog raced past the guards, carrying the Princess. A guard clutched at her. His fingers touched her foot and she was gone. But perhaps he pulled her slipper loose, because in the morning, when the Princess woke, it was gone.

"I dreamed I lost it and I have," she exclaimed happily.

"My dreams are real. My soldier is real!"

The King was less pleased. "Search everywhere, until you find the Princess's slipper," he told his guards. "And when you do, clap that upstart soldier in prison!"

Max was woken by guards bursting into the inn. The missing slipper was lying under his window. As soon as they saw it, they dragged him away. He didn't even have time to take the tinderbox.

The guards threw Max into a little stone cell and slammed the door. A key grated in the lock, and he was left all alone.

The cell was very dark and disagreeable, but thinking about the Princess gave Max hope. "If only I could get the tinderbox," he muttered. "I wonder..."

When one of the guards brought him dinner, Max begged for a candle. "It's so dark in here," he sighed.

"Candles are expensive," grumbled the guard.

"I have one at home – and a fine tinderbox to light it with – if you would only fetch it?"

The guard had a kind heart and was sorry to see such a brave young soldier in prison. So he took pity on Max and did as he asked.

As soon as Max set hands on the tinderbox, he struck it once, twice, thrice – until all three dogs appeared.

"Help me!" he cried.

The dogs roared, and the stones of the prison tumbled down. The guards all came running, only to see Max with the three dogs, racing away towards the copper castle.

The dogs roared again, and the copper walls crumpled like paper. The Princess came dashing towards him.

"My soldier!" she cried happily.

"My Princess!" answered Max, sweeping her off her feet.

The King trembled at the sight of the dogs. "I see I can't defeat fate," he admitted. "So I'd better make the most of it."

And to the young couple's delight, he gave Max half his kingdom and the Princess's hand in marriage.

The wedding celebrations lasted a whole week, and the dogs sat at the table and stared with their eyes like saucers, eyes like dinner plates and eyes like mill wheels. And Max and his beautiful bride lived happily ever after.

Twelve Dancing Princesses

Once upon a time, a King and Queen had twelve daughters, each more lovely than the last. The youngest, who was loveliest of all, they named Doralie. But soon after she was born, the Queen died. The King was heartbroken and, in his grief, he banned all music and dancing from the realm.

Years passed, and the Princesses grew older, but they never had any birthday parties or attended any royal balls. So imagine the King's astonishment when, one morning, all twelve Princesses came down to breakfast with their little satin slippers in tatters. The soles were worn right through.

"As if they'd spent all night dancing," muttered the King, frowning. "But how?"

The Princesses refused to say.

That night, when they went to bed, the King
locked their bedroom door behind them. But the next
day, twelve more pairs of ruined shoes met his eyes.

The night after that, the King locked the door *and*
doubled the guards. But in the morning, it was just the same.

At last the King made a royal decree: "If any man can
discover how the Princesses are wearing out their shoes, I will
give him half my kingdom and the hand of one of the Princesses
in marriage. But if he fails, he shall forfeit his life!"

Plenty of Princes rose to the challenge. They arrived with
fanfares and fine words. When night fell, they went to sit by
the Princesses' door. But somehow, as they watched and waited,
their eyes grew heavy – and in the morning, the Princesses'
shoes were worn through and the Princes were none the wiser.
So the King cast them into his dungeons to await their end.

The dungeons were almost full and the King was in despair,
when a young stranger turned up at the palace, carrying a
travel-stained cloak. "My name is Daniel," he announced. "And I
am here to discover what is happening to the Princesses' shoes."

The King sighed. "You know the price of failure," he said.
"What makes you think you will succeed?"

"I'm not afraid," said Daniel bravely. "I have my wits and my old cloak here, and that's enough for me."

That night, Daniel watched as, one by one, the Princesses went into their bedroom. Doralie blushed as she walked past, and Daniel caught his breath to see how lovely she looked. Then he settled down outside the door to wait.

Inside, the Princesses were talking quietly. Daniel listened.

"Can't we spare him?" pleaded Doralie. "He's so young and handsome!"

"And miss our fun tonight?" said the other Princesses. "Not likely!" Light footsteps came across the floor and the door opened. It was Delfina, the eldest Princess.

"Hello," she said politely. "You must be cold out there in the corridor. Would you like a hot drink?"

"Yes, please," said Daniel.

Delfina handed him a steaming goblet. Beyond her, Doralie caught her breath nervously.

"I wonder if this is what made the others fall asleep," thought Daniel. So he only pretended to drink. A moment later, he yawned and let his eyelids droop.

Delfina smiled and shut the door.

Now there was more whispering, quiet footsteps,
a rustling and a creak of hinges...

then silence.

Quick as a flash, Daniel threw on his old cloak –
and vanished! He hadn't told the King, but it was a
magic cloak, which made anyone who wore it invisible.

When Daniel opened the door, the bedroom was empty.
He glanced around and noticed a rug was slightly rumpled.
Underneath, he found a trapdoor to a secret staircase.
He followed the steps down into a tunnel lit by
flickering torches.

The Princesses were just ahead, dressed
as if for a ball. Doralie was last in line,
looking lovelier than ever in a rose-silk
gown with a long, trailing skirt.

Unwarily, Daniel stepped too close...

"Oh," exclaimed Doralie, looking all around.

"Someone pulled my dress!"

Delfina glanced back. "Don't be silly," she laughed.

"There's no one there. You must have caught it on a nail."

At last, the tunnel opened out into an underground forest.
Daniel's eyes widened in amazement. The trees had branches
of silver and leaves of gold, spangled all over with diamonds.

He reached out and broke off a branch – snap!

Doralie looked around. "Someone is following us," she insisted.

"Don't be silly," repeated Delfina impatiently. "You must have stepped on a twig."

Beyond the forest, a lake gleamed in the torchlight. Twelve boats waited on the shore, each with a Prince ready to row it across the water. On the far side, an enchanted castle stood invitingly, its windows ablaze with light.

Daniel jumped into Doralie's boat. Because her boat was heavier, the Prince rowed more slowly than usual.

"Something is different tonight," she muttered. But her sisters didn't listen.

Inside the castle, they entered a magnificent ballroom decorated all in silver and gold, and lit by diamond chandeliers. A band of musicians struck up a waltz, the Princes bowed to the Princesses, and they began to dance together, whirling and twirling over the polished gold floor.

It was a beautiful spectacle, but Daniel had eyes only for Doralie, with her long curls and dimpled smile. As she swept past, her cheeks flushed and eyes sparkling, it was clear how much she loved to dance.

"I wish *I* was dancing with her," thought Daniel.

The Princesses danced and danced, until their satin slippers were worn right through. And then they had to leave.

Daniel followed as they crossed back over the lake, through the wood, along the tunnel and up the steps into their bedroom – where they flung off their ruined shoes and fell asleep, smiling.

Back outside their door, Daniel smiled too. "I've done it," he thought happily.

The next morning, Doralie watched anxiously as Daniel stood before the King.

"Well?" said the King.

"Your Majesty, I have discovered the answer," declared Daniel boldly. And he described everything he had seen.

"Do you have proof?"

In answer, Daniel pulled out a silver branch tipped with golden leaves, and glittering all over with diamonds. It sparkled so brightly, it made the room dance with light.

"It's true," sighed the King. "You have earned the reward – half my kingdom and a Princess's hand in marriage.

But which Princess?"

Daniel caught Doralie's eye, and she blushed.

"Little Doralie," he said. "If she will have me."

Doralie smiled. "Willingly," she said softly.

"There'll be no more dancing now you've revealed our secret," sniffed Delfina.

"Oh, but I shall insist on dancing at the wedding!" Daniel told her. He turned to the King. "And you'll have to let all those Princes out of your dungeons, and invite the Princes from the enchanted castle, so the Princesses will have plenty of dancing partners."

The wedding was a huge success. Daniel hired the finest musicians, and the Princesses danced to their hearts' content – and maybe there was magic in the air, for the King suddenly remembered how much he loved dancing too. He danced with his daughters, they danced with the Princes, and Doralie and Daniel danced with each other, as happy as they could be.

And they all lived happily ever after.

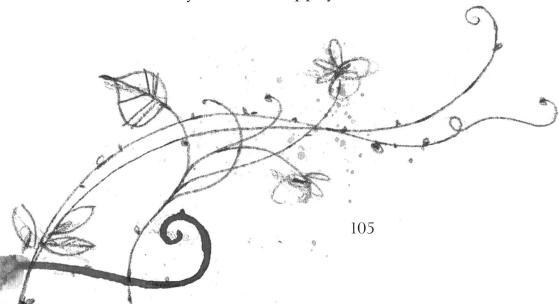

Puss in Boots

There was once a poor miller who died, leaving his
three sons nothing but a tumbledown mill, a stubborn
old donkey and a stripey cat. The oldest son claimed the mill,
and the middle son took the donkey – so all that was left
for the youngest son, Peppo, was the cat.

It was a very handsome cat, with tawny stripes like a tiger –
but Peppo couldn't help feeling disappointed.

"My brothers can earn their living by grinding corn
and carrying it to market," he said to himself. "But I've got
nothing except an extra mouth to feed!"

He sighed and stroked the cat's ears.

"What shall we do together, Puss?"

107

Puss closed his emerald eyes and purrrrrred.

"We will do verrry well, if you will trust me," he said.

"You can talk!" cried Peppo.

"Yes, and many other things besides," answered Puss calmly. "We won't go hungry."

Puss was right – each day, he caught them a nice, fat fish or rabbit for dinner. Sometimes, when there were too many mice, Peppo hired Puss (who was a talented mouser) to the local villagers, in exchange for a few coins. And so they got by, and even saved a little.

One day, as they were coming back from the village, a carriage swept past them, drawn by six high-stepping horses. The driver and footmen wore velvet coats, and there was a golden crown on the door. But Peppo had eyes only for the passenger – a lady with warm brown eyes and an even warmer smile. "Who was that?" he sighed.

"The King's daughter, Perlita," Puss told him.

"A princess," said Peppo and he stared sadly at his feet.

Puss grinned. "You're in love!" he mewed.

"How can I love a princess – me, a poor miller's son?" retorted Peppo. But he blushed.

"I'll help," promised Puss. "I think I know a way to introduce you. But first, I need a suit and boots."

Peppo immediately gathered up their savings and went to see the tailor.

A few days later, Puss had a dashing new suit, with a feathered hat and shiny new boots to match. He tried them on and took a few swaggering steps in front of the mirror. His whiskers twitched as he smiled.

"Verrry handsome," he purred. "Even if I do say so myself.

Now, for my plan..."

He went down to the river and fished until he caught a fine, fat salmon. But, instead of taking it home to Peppo, he straightened his suit and marched boldly up to the palace.

"A present for the King, from the Marquis of Catanza," he mewed loudly.

The next day, Puss went out into the fields and snared a hare, and took that to the palace. "A present from the Marquis of Catanza," he said again.

The day after that, he went into the woods and caught a pair of plump partridges... "A present from the Marquis of Catanza," he repeated.

"You again," cried the guards. "His Majesty has asked to see you! He's very curious about these gifts." And they led Puss to the throne room.

Puss swaggered in, swept off his hat and bowed. "Your Majesty," he purred politely.

"A talking cat!" cried the King. "What a marvel."

"It's nothing compared to the marvels of my master's castle," said Puss. "I work for the Marquis of Catanza."

"Who is he?" asked the King.

"You don't know the Marquis? A man famous for his good looks, great talent and even greater fortune?"

"Er, no," admitted the King. "But I'd be delighted to meet him, if he would like to visit me."

Puss went home very well pleased.

"Visit the palace?" exclaimed Peppo, when Puss told him about the invite. "Impossible!" He glanced down at his rags. "I can't go like this – and I spent my last penny on your boots."

"Never mind," said Puss. "I'll arrange everything."

"Just remember to answer to the name, the Marquis of Catanza. Let me see... first, you should have a bath in the river."

As soon as Peppo had undressed and dived in, Puss took all of his clothes.

"Hey," cried Peppo. "What are you doing?"

Puss pretended not to hear. He hid the clothes under a rock, then ran all the way to the palace.

"Help, help!" he cried breathlessly. "Thieves have attacked the Marquis, stolen his clothes and thrown him in the river to drown."

"Good gracious," cried the King, ordering his servants to go to the rescue. "And take some of my spare clothes for the Marquis to wear," he added.

So Peppo went to the palace dressed like a king, and squeaky clean after his long soak. He looked very handsome and the Princess kept glancing shyly in his direction.

The King had ordered a great feast for Peppo's visit, with roast boar and baked partridge and grilled trout, a dozen different desserts, and a whole bowlful of cream for Puss. Peppo had never known such luxury – though Puss kept telling everyone it was nothing compared to the Marquis's home life.

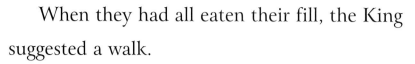

When they had all eaten their fill, the King
suggested a walk.

"Grrreat," purred Puss. "Now I can show you all
the wonderful things belonging to my master, the Marquis."

"Puss, what are you doing?" hissed Peppo, looking perplexed.
"I don't own anything!"

"Don't worry," replied Puss quietly. "I have a plan.
Just remember to act like a Marquis."

They strolled out of the palace and Puss ran on ahead.
Before long, he met a man with a flock of sheep.

"Pssst," hissed Puss. "There are some robbers coming down
the road – don't let their fine appearances fool you! They've
already robbed the palace, now they're looking for more loot.
They'd love to steal your sheep! Your only hope is to say they
belong to the Marquis of Catanza. If they hear that, they will
leave you alone."

Then the King and Peppo caught up. "What fine sheep,"
said the King. "Who do they belong to?"

"The Marquis of Catanza," said the man hastily.
"They all belong to him."

Peppo stared. "How does Puss do it?" he thought.

They went on, Puss running ahead as before. Puss told everyone he met about the 'robbers'. So whenever the King asked who owned this pair of prancing horses or that herd of contented cows, these orchards of rosy apples or those fields of golden corn, he always heard the same reply – "The Marquis of Catanza."

"My dear Marquis, I must congratulate you," said the King, very much impressed with it all.

Then they saw a grand castle. Puss turned to the King and bowed. "As we're passing, I'm sure my master would like to invite you to see his home."

"How lovely," said the King.

"I'll just run ahead and tell the servants," said Puss.

"B-b-but," stuttered Peppo, not seeing how even Puss could manage this – but Puss had already raced off.

Now, the castle didn't belong to Peppo, as we all know. Really it belonged to a fearsome ogre. And the sheep and horses and cows and apples and corn the King had admired belonged to him as well. The ogre was very rich and very mean... and not very pleased to find a strange cat grinning up at him.

"What are you doing here?" he growled.

"Oh great ogre, I bring greetings from the King himself,"
said Puss, with a deep bow. "We have heard so much about your
magical powers, the King has sent me to ask – is it true you
can change yourself into anything you want?"

"Watch me," snapped the ogre. He waved one hand
and in a flash, instead of an ogre, there was a huge grizzly
bear with savage teeth and claws. He stared at Puss,
opened slavering jaws and gave a ferocious

ROAR!

Puss trembled. "Very good," he
squeaked. "Just like a real bear."

The bear smiled smugly and, with a wave of a huge paw, became an ogre again.

"Amazing," said Puss. "You certainly make an impressive bear. But I bet you can't do small animals. Say, for example, a mouse – surely you can't make yourself so tiny."

"Of course I can," huffed the ogre, waving his hand again and shrinking rapidly... until a little brown mouse stood in his place, twitching its whiskers with satisfaction.

Puss grinned – and pounced.

By the time the King and Peppo arrived, Puss had lined up all the ogre's servants and told them to welcome their new master, the Marquis of Catanza.

"The Marquis is a very kind man – look what fine boots he gave me," he told them. "Make him and the King welcome, and you'll never want for anything again."

That night, the whole castle echoed with the sounds of celebrations. The servants were thrilled the ogre was gone, the King was delighted with his new friend, the Marquis – and the Marquis was ecstatic, because the beautiful Princess Perlita was dancing with him.

"Will you marry me?" he whispered, as they whirled across the ballroom together.

"Willingly," she said, with her warmest smile.

So Peppo and Perlita were married and lived happily ever after in the castle. As for Puss, the grateful Peppo saw to it that he had a suit and boots for every day of the week and dined off salmon and cream – and he never chased another mouse again, except for fun.

East of the Sun, West of the Moon

Once upon a time, there was a poor farmer who had so many children, he could hardly afford to feed them. But he loved them all dearly, especially his daughter, Elsa, with her bright eyes and kind heart.

They lived in the north, where the winters are bitter and long. One cold, snowy evening, there was a knock at the door. The farmer answered it – and found himself face-to-face with a huge white bear. It had a tousled white coat and strong white paws and, when it opened its jaws, the farmer thought his last day had come. But then, to his astonishment, he realized the bear was speaking.

"You are poor," growled the bear. "But I can make you rich, if you will give me your daughter."

The farmer shook his head. "Never!" he said.

But the bear did not give up. "Think it over," he roared, padding away. "I'll be back tomorrow."

Elsa had heard everything. "I can make sure my family never wants for anything," she thought. "It's up to me."

So the next night, she secretly slipped outside. When the bear came back, she was waiting for him.

"Climb onto my back and hold tight," rumbled the bear. "Are you afraid?"

"No," answered Elsa boldly. And she thought she saw the bear smile. Then, they set off into the night.

The bear carried her fast and far,
through snowy forests. At last they stopped beside a
stone tower. Inside, Elsa found a delicious dinner waiting
on a silver tray, stacks of beautiful books to read, and a vast
four-poster bed with soft silk sheets. It was more luxury than
she could ever have imagined.

"If only Father could see me now," she sighed, putting out
the lamp and getting into bed. A few moments later, the door
creaked open – and she heard someone flop down on the floor!

121

"Bear, is that you?" asked Elsa nervously.

The only answer was a low, rumbling snore – but it was a gentle, friendly sort of snore. Whoever it was had gone straight to sleep. And before long, Elsa was asleep too.

In the morning, there was no sign of anyone, but the same thing happened the next night, and the next...

During the day, Elsa spent her time reading and talking to the bear – and grew very fond of him. But she couldn't help feeling homesick from time to time.

"You look sad," the bear told her one day.

"I miss my family," she replied.

"Then you shall visit them," said the bear. "But if they try to give you advice, don't listen! No good will come of it."

The bear carried her back to her old home – and it was much changed. The run-down old cottage was transformed into a handsome house, and her brothers were playing outside. They shouted with delight when they saw her, and asked her all about her new life.

When she described the mysterious nighttime snores, her father frowned.

"It could be anyone," he said sternly. "Even a troll or a monster!"

"Take my advice: hide a candle under your pillow, wait for him to fall asleep and take a good long look."

Elsa shook her head, remembering the bear's warning. But she was very, very curious. "I'm sure it can't hurt just to look," she thought. So when the bear came to take her back, she had a candle concealed in her pocket.

That night, Elsa quietly lit the candle, and gasped. There, on the floor, lay a handsome Prince – and there was something familiar about him. He had tousled white-blonde hair and strong-looking hands.

"Bear?" whispered Elsa. As she leaned over to look more closely, three drops of candle wax fell onto his shirt.

The Prince woke with a start. "Oh no," he cried. "If only you had waited. A witch turned me into a bear because I refused to marry her, but at night I am human again. To break the spell, I had to live beside you for a year without you seeing my true face. Now I must return to the witch and marry her."

"No!" cried Elsa, suddenly realizing how much she loved him. "I won't let that happen! There must be another way to break the spell."

"There might be one," said the Prince. "But it won't be easy."

"What must I do?" begged Elsa.

"Come to the witch's castle," the Prince told her. "East of the sun and west of the moon…" But before he could say any more, he vanished – and the tower vanished with him.

Elsa was alone in the snow.

"East of the sun and west of the moon," Elsa repeated sadly, as a gentle wind ruffled her hair. "How can I find such a place?"

"East," whispered a voice. "West… the Winds know best. Don't give up, child." It was the East Wind.

"I don't know the place myself," went on the East Wind. "But one of my brothers is sure to have been there." And he called out to them.

"East of the sun?" puffed the West Wind. "Never heard of it."

"West of the moon?" sighed the South Wind.

"It's too far for me."

"I saw it once," howled the North Wind. "It's at the very top of the world. Come, I'll show you." He took Elsa's hand and whirled her up in a chilly gust of air.

They blew swiftly along, until they reached the frozen lands at the top of the world. A gloomy castle loomed out of the snow.

"There!" cried Elsa, pointing, and the North Wind set her gently down.

A door banged open, revealing a long-nosed witch.

"Who's there?" she snapped. "What do you want?"

Elsa thought quickly.

"I heard you need a wedding gown," she said. "I can make one for you."

"Come in," cackled the witch eagerly. She took Elsa into a little dark sewing room, and left her there to work.

As soon as Elsa was alone, she stole away to look for the Prince. She found him sitting sadly by himself. But when he saw Elsa, he jumped up and gave her a hug worthy of a bear.

"You made it!" he cried in delight. "Now we can defeat the witch, for love is more than a match for magic.

Listen, I've got a plan..."

The next day, the Prince went to see the witch.

"My shirt has some spots of wax on it," he told her.

"I'll happily marry the woman who cleans it!"

"Very well," snapped the witch. "That's easy."

But as soon as she touched the shirt, the spots grew darker.
Angrily, she tried to magic them away, but the stains only grew
bigger and blacker.

"You'd better let someone else try," laughed the Prince,
tossing the shirt to Elsa. In her hands, the cloth turned as white
as snow – and the witch's spell was broken. The witch screeched
with fury and vanished.

"Now," said the Prince, "I said I'd marry the woman
who cleaned my shirt. Elsa, may I keep my word?"

"Oh yes," replied Elsa, grinning.

So a few days later, they were married in Elsa's father's
garden, on a sunny day without a breath of wind – for all
four Winds were guests at the wedding.

FEARLESS HANS

Hans lived an ordinary sort of life, in an ordinary sort of house – but he was not an ordinary sort of boy. Nothing made him afraid, not scary stories, not the dark, not spiders or snakes or things that go bump in the night.

And so his friends called him Fearless Hans.

One day, Hans was out playing with his friends when the wind rose, and huge drops of rain began to fall. There was a flicker of lightning, followed by a fearsome sound, as if the sky was tearing itself apart. The other children ran home, frightened. Hans followed behind them, wondering what on earth was going on.

"Shut the door," cried his mother, as he came in.

"The thunder makes me shiver."

"I'd like to shiver," thought Hans. He sat down and listened carefully to the thunderclaps, but nothing happened.

He was still sitting there when his father came home.

"What are you doing?" asked his father.

"Trying to shiver," said Hans. "Oh, I wish I could."

"That's easy," laughed his father. "You just need a good fright. Leave it to me!" He sent Hans out to fetch some firewood. While Hans was gone, he dressed up as a ghost and hid behind the door.

When Hans came back, loaded with sticks, a billowing white figure leaped out at him. "Who are you?" asked Hans curiously. "And what are you doing here?"

The ghost didn't answer, but moaned and groaned and reached out its arms...

"I can see you're up to no good," said Hans. "But I'll soon get rid of you." And he seized the biggest stick and began to beat the creature back.

"Ow!" yelled the ghost, in a familiar voice. Then his father emerged from under a sheet, bruised and cross. "It's no good," he snapped. "You'll have to do this by yourself."

So Hans left home, to learn how to shiver. While he walked, he sighed over and over, "Oh, I wish I could shiver!"

Eventually, he met an old farmer who lived in the hills.

"Oh, I wish I could shiver," said Hans.

"Then I know just the place for you," said the farmer. He pointed to a craggy peak that towered above the other hills. "That mountain makes me shiver just thinking about it!"

"Why is that?" asked Hans eagerly.

"Because of the terrible troll that lives there," replied the farmer, with a shudder. "They say it *eats* people!"

"Thank you," cried Hans, and he set off at once.

The mountaintop was dark and desolate, littered with rocks and old bones, but Hans was not afraid.

"Fee, fie, fo, fum..." boomed a stony voice. "I hear the steps of a shivering man!" It was the troll.

"But I'm not shivering," complained Hans.

The troll rolled a lopsided ball towards him. When Hans picked it up, he saw it was a skull.

"Are you shivering now?" demanded the troll.

"No," said Hans. "But I see your ball needs a bit of work. Let me polish it for you."

He whittled and polished, until the skull was quite smooth, and then he rolled it back. "There, that's better."

The troll scratched its head uncertainly.

"Fee, fie, fo, fum," it tried again. "Alive and shivering, or cold and dead, I'll grind your bones to make my bread."

"Bread?" echoed Hans. "It's nice of you to offer. I could do with a bit of bread after my journey." He looked around, found the remains of a loaf and tried to take a bite. "Oof!"

The bread was as hard as rock. But he didn't want to seem rude, so he pretended to eat it while secretly stuffing the rest under his shirt.

The troll growled. Then, it picked up a knife and tried to stab Hans. Hans dodged – but the tip of the knife caught his shirt, and bits of bread scattered across the floor.

The troll stared. "I cut you open, but you're still alive."

Hans thought quickly. "Oh, it's no use attacking me," he said. "I'm so strong, no wound can hurt me."

"But you're not as strong as me," said the troll boastfully. "Look!" And with that, it stabbed itself – and dropped down dead.

When people found out that Hans had defeated the troll, he was celebrated as a great hero.

The troll's cave turned out to be full of treasure – so Hans became rich, too. But he still didn't know what it was like to shiver.

Eventually, after he married, his wife became fed up with hearing him sigh – "Oh, I wish I could shiver!"

So early one morning, while Hans was still asleep, she fetched a bucketful of eels – cold, wet, wriggly eels – and tipped them into his bed.

Hans woke up, quivering and shivering, among the slithering eels. "My wonderful wife," he cried, jumping up and hugging her.

"You've done what no one else could do...

now, at last, I know how to shiver!"

BEAUTY AND THE BEAST

Far away and long ago, there was a merchant with three daughters. The merchant had once been rich, but he had fallen on hard times, and the older girls spent their days complaining about the fine clothes and jewels they had lost. Only the youngest, Belle, did her best to be happy and to make the others so.

One day, the merchant had to go away on business. Before he left, he asked his daughters if they would like him to bring anything back for them.

Two of the sisters exchanged greedy glances.

"A gold brooch," said one grandly.

"A pearl necklace," added the other quickly.

"And you, Belle?" insisted the merchant.

Belle didn't want to ask for anything so costly. She glanced
at their empty garden. "I'd love a rose," she said softly.

The merchant rode away. It was a long trip and he was gone
for several days. But he didn't forget his daughters. With his
small stock of coins, he bought a little gold brooch and a string
of tiny seed pearls – but it was late in the year and there were
no roses anywhere.

As he set off for home, icy rain stung his face. He pulled up
his collar and rode on, into a frozen forest. Then a thick mist
rose up, so that he could hardly see the road ahead. Before long
he was completely lost.

A light glimmered in the mist and he rode towards it. The air
grew warmer. Then, the mist rolled back and he found himself
in the garden of a magnificent castle, bathed in golden sunshine.

"What is this place?" he gasped.

Leaving his horse contentedly grazing the grass, he climbed
the steps to a huge oak door.

Before he could knock, the door swung open by itself.

"Hello! Is anyone there?" he called. There was no reply.

Inside, he found a hall lit by flickering torches and a flaming fire. Beside the fire stood a comfortable chair and a table spread with food. Suddenly, he realized how tired he was.

He sat down, and invisible hands pushed a plate in front of him. Too hungry to be afraid, he ate.

When he had eaten his fill, the merchant went looking for his host. "I must thank someone," he thought.

The castle rooms were echoing and empty, so he went out into the garden. But, apart from many wild birds and animals, there was no sign of life.

At the end of one path, he smelled a sweet, familiar scent. "Roses!" The rich velvet blooms filled a whole flowerbed. "Belle would love these."

He reached out a hand. *Snap*, went a stem. And then came an ear-rending RRRR-ROAR!

An enormous beast sprang out from the bushes. It was dressed like a man but looked more like a lion, with a tangled mane of hair and savage teeth. The merchant trembled.

Eyes blazing, the creature pointed a clawed finger at him.

"Miserable human, how dare you steal my flowers? Is it not enough that I give you food and shelter? And this is how you repay my kindness. You deserve to die!"

"I'm s-s-sorry, sir," the merchant replied, through chattering teeth. "I m-m-meant no harm. After your generosity, I n-n-never thought you would mind the loss of so small a thing."

"Fine words," snarled the creature. "But my name is Beast, not *sir*, and you shall die for your greed."

"It was not for myself I picked it," the merchant said hastily, "but my daughter, Belle."

The Beast paused. "You have a daughter..." It rubbed a hairy cheek. "Would she love you enough to take your place?"

"I couldn't ask her to do that," cried the merchant.

The Beast ignored him. "I'll give you a week. After that, you must send me your daughter or return to meet your fate! Give me your word."

Reluctantly, the merchant nodded.

"Your horse knows the way," growled the Beast. "Now go!"

The merchant did not wait to be told twice. He hurried back to his horse. As soon as he swung into the saddle, it set off so swiftly that he could scarcely tell what path they took, but they were soon home.

Belle greeted her father with a smile and a hug.
"I'm so glad you're back," she told him.

"Did you get our presents?" interrupted her sisters.

"Yes," said the merchant, pulling out the jewels and one
perfect rose. He stared at it sadly. "But at such a cost..."

Belle paled as she heard what had happened in the forest.

"Why don't you shoot the wretch?" snapped her sisters.
"You can't keep such a bargain."

"I must," sighed the merchant. "I gave my word – and I
think the Beast has the power to hold me to it."

The sisters turned on Belle. "This is all your fault!"

"I never thought a rose would cost so dear," she replied
quietly. "But if this is the price, then *I* must pay it."

"No," said the merchant shakily. "I won't let you. I only
came back to say goodbye." A tear rolled down his lined face.
Belle embraced him, but her mind was made up.

The next morning, she woke early and wrote a note.

Dear Father,
I've gone to meet the Beast.
Don't cry for me.
Belle.

Then she saddled her father's horse.

"Take me to the Beast," she whispered.

It whinnied and set off as swiftly as before.

Before long, they were flying through the icy forest.
Mist curled thickly about the trees and Belle shivered – but then
the air grew warmer. The mist cleared and she saw they were
galloping up a grassy avenue towards a towering castle.

The horse stopped before a grand oak entrance.
Belle climbed the steps. The door swung open and she went on,
into the torchlit hall. There was the chair by the fire and there
was the table, loaded with pastries, fruit and all the things she
usually loved to eat. But she had no appetite.

"I wonder if the Beast plans to kill me?" she thought. "Still, I'm here now, so I must be brave. And perhaps the Beast will be more gentle when he is less angry." So she sat down to wait.

Eventually, she heard footsteps. Her heart quailed at the sight of the Beast, but she smiled politely. "Good day, Beast."

"Good day, Belle," growled the Beast. "I am glad to see you! I have been very lonely here. Will you stay with me?"

"Y-yes," said Belle.

"I am glad," rumbled the Beast, and his lips twitched in what might have been a smile. "Have you looked around?"

Belle shook her head.

"The castle is yours to enjoy," the Beast told her. "Go where you like, do as you please. I ask only that you eat dinner with me each night."

"Thank you," said Belle, surprised. "You are very kind."

The Beast nodded and left her alone again.

Belle breathed a sigh of relief and set off to explore.

She discovered sitting rooms full of soft couches and cushions, a music room with every kind of instrument, and a library with all the books she had ever heard of and many more she hadn't. But there was no sign of any other inhabitant.

One room was lined with mirrors. To her amazement, as she looked, the glass shimmered and changed to reflect bustling streets, sparkling seascapes, and even a familiar study where a merchant sat sighing over a crumpled note...

"Father!" Suddenly, she felt less alone.

Then she saw a door with *Belle* written on it. As she looked, it swung open to reveal a prettily furnished bedroom. There was a four-poster bed, a wardrobe filled with silk and satin dresses, a box of jewels lying open on a dressing table, and even a tame songbird which chirruped softly in greeting...

"The Beast is very kind to go to so much trouble," she told herself, gently stroking the bird's crest.

Something caught her eye among the jewels. It was a silver locket, with a portrait of a handsome Prince inside. Belle gazed at his kind smile. Then she slipped the locket around her neck and, because she was very tired, she lay down on the bed and fell fast asleep.

In her sleep, she dreamed the Prince stood before her and spoke. "Do not be afraid, Belle. All is not as it seems."

"I wonder what he means," she thought. But before she could ask him, a clock chimed and she woke up.

"Dinnertime," realized Belle, jumping up. She found the Beast waiting for her in the hall, where the table was laid ready. She bid him good evening and they sat down to eat.

To Belle's surprise, the Beast proved an agreeable companion. His manners were as gentle as his face was fierce.

"Did you find everything to your liking?" he asked.

"Can you be happy here?"

"Oh yes, thank you," said Belle.

The Beast smiled. Belle was just beginning to think he wasn't so bad when he asked a question which set her heart pounding.

"Belle, will you marry me?"

"No, Beast," she said firmly. "Now he'll be angry!" she thought. But the Beast just bowed his head sadly and left her alone in the hall.

Now Belle spent her days as she pleased, reading or playing music, or exploring the castle and garden. Invisible hands brought her whatever she wished, and she lacked for nothing. In the evenings, she had dinner with the Beast, and enjoyed their conversations. Always, before he left, he asked the same question. "Belle, will you marry me?"

And always, she gave the same answer. "No, Beast."

One day, the Beast asked if there was anything that could make her happier.

Belle hesitated. "I would like to visit my family."

The Beast heaved a great sigh. "Ah, Belle, I cannot refuse you. But I fear you will not return."

"Oh no!" cried Belle. "I'll be back in a week, I promise."

"Take this," said the Beast, holding out a strangely carved ring. "It will transport you wherever you wish. It will carry you home, and back here again – if you wish it."

"Thank you!" cried Belle, slipping on the ring. "I wish I was at home." She saw the Beast gazing sorrowfully at her, and then the room whirled around her. She closed her eyes...

...and when she opened them again, her father was gazing at her in delight. "Belle!" he cried. "I've been so worried."

"You don't need to be," she laughed. And she told her family all about the Beast's kindness and life in the castle.

When Belle's sisters heard what luxury she enjoyed, their eyes narrowed. "It's not fair," they told each other. "Belle never cared for fine things. It should be one of us in that castle!"

Mad with jealousy, they began to plot. "If we make Belle break her promise, the Beast will be angry with her!" said one.

"He might even eat her up!" put in the other.
"And then he'll need a new companion..."

So they begged Belle to stay. "Just a few more days,"
they wailed, when it was time for her to go. "We *need* you!"
And they sobbed crocodile tears until reluctantly, Belle agreed.

That night, Belle dreamed she was walking in the castle
garden when she heard groans. It was the Beast. He was
slumped on the ground, his mane tangled and his eyes dim.

"Belle," he sighed. "Why did you forsake me?"

All at once, Belle knew he was dying. And then she woke.
"Oh Beast," she sobbed. "I'm so sorry! I'll come at once."
She clutched the ring and wished with all her might...

Suddenly, she was back at the castle, running through the
dusky garden. "Beast, where are you?" Twigs tore her hair and
stones scratched her feet, but she hardly noticed.

He was lying on the ground, just like in her dream. His eyes
were closed and he was hardly breathing.

Timidly, she stroked his mane. "Beast," she whispered.

His eyelids flickered. "You came back," he growled.
"Thank you. Now I can die beside the one I love."

"Beast," she wept. "Oh Beast, don't die. I love you!"

He breathed more deeply. "Belle, will you marry me?"

"Yes, Beast!"

The Beast smiled – and as he smiled, his mane and claws began to shrivel and shrink. His face transformed... Belle touched the silver locket she wore. "It's you," she said. "You're the Prince I saw!"

"Yes," he replied. "I was under a spell, but you have set me free. Thank you! Long ago, I offended a fairy and she made me into the Beast, until I could find someone to love me."

They walked back to the castle, arm-in-arm. Overhead, fireworks fizzed and popped, filling the sky with gold and silver stars. More bright stars were flitting in and out of the castle. Belle looked closer... "Fairies!" she exclaimed.

"Yes," the Prince told her. "They look after the castle, but you can only see them now the spell is broken."

The wedding was held a few days later. All of Belle's family came to see it – and the fairies came too, to see that everything turned out right. They smiled at Belle's father, and restored his fortune with a wave of their wands. But they frowned upon the selfish sisters.

"Such stony hearts deserve to be turned to stone," said the oldest fairy. "At least until they learn better!" And with another wave, two new statues appeared in the garden.

As for Belle and her Prince –

"May you live happily ever after," the fairies told them.

And they did.

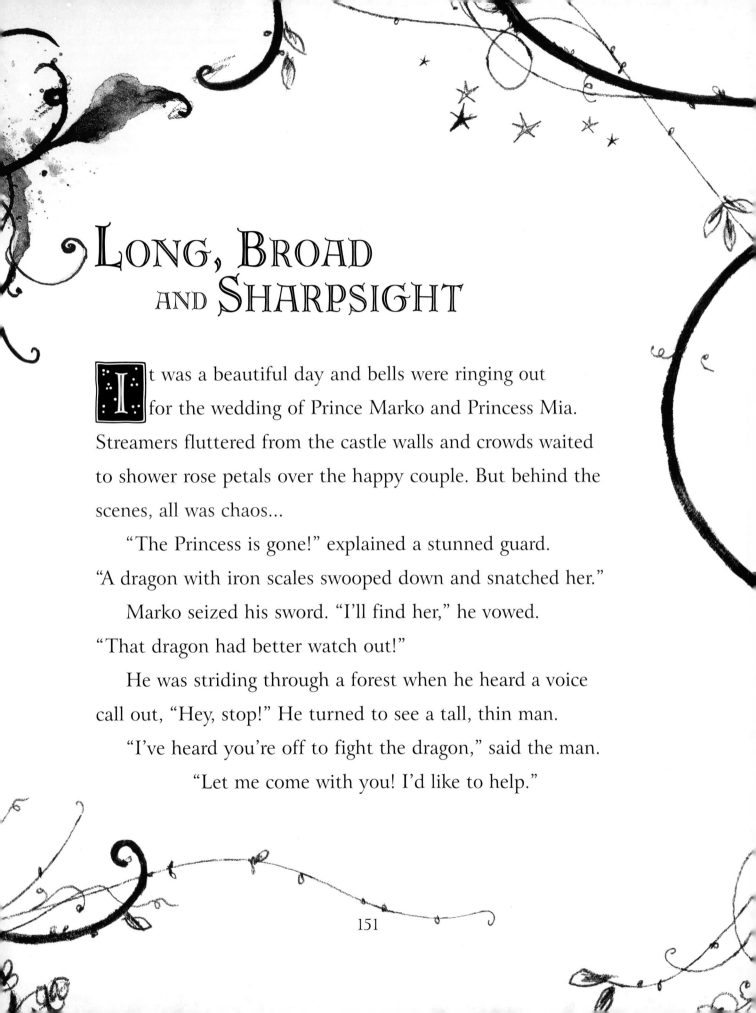

Long, Broad and Sharpsight

It was a beautiful day and bells were ringing out for the wedding of Prince Marko and Princess Mia. Streamers fluttered from the castle walls and crowds waited to shower rose petals over the happy couple. But behind the scenes, all was chaos...

"The Princess is gone!" explained a stunned guard. "A dragon with iron scales swooped down and snatched her."

Marko seized his sword. "I'll find her," he vowed. "That dragon had better watch out!"

He was striding through a forest when he heard a voice call out, "Hey, stop!" He turned to see a tall, thin man.

"I've heard you're off to fight the dragon," said the man. "Let me come with you! I'd like to help."

"Thank you," replied Marko. "But what can you do? It's not easy fighting dragons."

"That's why you need me," insisted the man. "My name is Long, and I can make myself as long as I please. Look!" He stretched up, growing taller and taller, until he towered above the treetops. Startled pigeons flew away in all directions.

Marko stared. "Very well! You can be my lookout."

Long smiled. "At the edge of the forest, I spy my friend Broad. You should bring him along, too."

"Call him over."

"He's too far away to hear me. I'll have to fetch him."

Long strode off, his long legs stepping easily over the trees. Moments later, he was back with a short, round man.

"What can *you* do?" said Marko curiously.

"I'll show you," said Broad. "If you stand back."

When the others were at a safe distance, he drew a deep breath, puffing himself up until he was as broad as a mountain. There was a terrible grinding and snapping as trees broke around him. Then, he breathed out. Wind howled around their ears and blew through the forest like a gale.

"Great," gasped Marko. "I'd be glad to have you along."

Broad grinned. "Through the trees, I see my friend Sharpsight wearing a blindfold. You should bring him too."

"What's wrong with his eyes?" asked Marko.

"Nothing," replied Sharpsight, coming over. "On the contrary, I can see just as well as you, even with this blindfold. Without it, I can see right through things or even... watch!"

He lifted the blindfold, revealing a piercing blue gaze, and stared at a nearby rock. The rock smoked and sizzled and shattered into pieces.

"Amazing!" exclaimed Marko. "I'd be glad of your help. Tell me, Sharpsight, can you see Princess Mia?"

Sharpsight gazed at the horizon. "Yes," he said. "She is a prisoner in an iron castle, many leagues from here. But with Long's help, we can be there by nightfall."

Long scooped them all up and set off, his long legs taking huge strides. Hills and valleys whizzed by, until they came to a mountain that was so big, even Long could not step over it.

"Leave this to me," said Sharpsight. He uncovered his eyes and glared at the rocky slope, until it cracked apart. Through the gap they saw a dark, glassy lake and, on a small, wooded island, a castle built of iron. "There," cried Sharpsight.

On the shore of the lake was an old sailing boat, but its sail hung slack and useless in the still air. "Come on," said Broad. When they were all aboard, he took a deep breath and whooooosh!

He sent them speeding over the water.

As they drew nearer the island, they heard a hideous clanking. "It's the trees," realized Marko with surprise, peering at their rusty leaves. "They're made of iron, too."

Nervously, they entered the castle through iron doors, into a hall full of iron figures, frozen in the middle of an iron feast.

At one end, a slender figure sat on a throne, pale-faced amid the gloom. "Mia!" She didn't look up or answer, but something moved in the shadows beyond. Marko gripped his sword, expecting to see the dragon. But no – it was a man, with a cloak of iron scales and three belts around his waist.

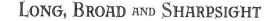

Long let out a hiss. "That's a shape-shifting magician," he whispered. "*He* carried off the Princess, not a real dragon at all!"

"So the Prince has come to rescue his bride," sneered the magician. "How brave. Well, I shall set you a challenge. If she is at your side in the morning for three days, I will let her go. If you fail, I will turn you to iron like all these other fools." And he waved a hand at the iron figures around the hall.

Marko squared his shoulders. "Very well."

"Let the challenge begin," cried the magician – and vanished.

Now the companions had to decide how to guard the Princess. Marko sat holding her hand, his sword at the ready. Sharpsight stood at the window, keeping lookout. Broad puffed himself up in the doorway, until it was sealed tight. And Long wrapped himself around and around the room.

They meant to stay awake all night, but there was magic at work and, one by one, their heads drooped. Marko woke at dawn, to find himself holding – nothing! Mia had vanished. Fear cut him like a knife. "Wake up," he hissed.

Sharpsight gazed out of the window, rubbing the sleep from his eyes. "I see her," he said. "The magician has turned her into an acorn in an oak tree, a hundred miles from here."

"We'll get her," said Long, taking Sharpsight and striding away. Moments later, they were back with an acorn. They put it down and, in a flash, it turned back into the Princess.

At the same time, the magician threw open the door. Crash! His face turned red with anger and one of his belts snapped.

"Two days to go," he snapped.

After a long day of waiting, the companions took up their posts again. And again, their eyes grew heavy and they fell asleep, only to wake and find the Princess gone.

Sharpsight stared furiously out of the window. "She's a diamond in the heart of a mountain, two hundred miles away."

"We can get her," said Long, taking Sharpsight and racing off. "If you split open the mountain for me."

They were barely back when the door was flung wide. Crash! The glittering gem turned back into the Princess and the magician's face contorted with fury. "You haven't succeeded yet," he hissed, as a second belt snapped.

After another day of waiting, they took up watch for the third time. This time, they paced up and down, and pinched themselves – but still their eyes closed. Marko awoke at dawn to an empty throne. "Quick, Sharpsight – where is she?"

Sharpsight scanned the horizon. "I can't see her! No, wait
– there, at the bottom of the sea, she's a pearl inside a seashell!
We'll have to make haste, it's three hundred miles off, and we'll
need Broad's help this time."

Long picked up Sharpsight and Broad, and sprinted away.
When they reached the sea, Broad began gulping down water.

"Ugh, salty!" he grimaced.

As soon as the water was low enough, Long ran out and
scooped up the shell. Inside was a perfect, round pearl.

"Hurry," warned Sharpsight. "The sun is nearly up."

Back at the castle, Marko was gazing anxiously out of
the window. "Where are they?" he muttered.

Crash! The magician appeared in the doorway with a
triumphant laugh. But before he could speak, there was
another crash. The window shattered and a shining pearl
fell at his feet, and then the Princess was standing there.
Sharpsight had spied the danger from afar and told
Long, who had thrown the pearl.

The magician's laugh became a howl of fury and his third belt snapped. Finally, his power was broken. With the last of his strength, he turned himself into a dragon and flew out of the shattered window.

At last, Mia raised her eyes and smiled. "My Prince!" she cried, rushing into Marko's welcoming arms. At the same time, a fresh green stole across the trees, the figures in the hall shook off their rust, and the castle filled with life and light – just as it had been before the magician came.

Marko turned to his companions. "How can I thank you?"

"There's no need," they replied, smiling. "We love adventures – especially ones with happy endings."

So Prince Marko and Princess Mia were married and lived happily for the rest of their days, and no one ever saw the magician again. As for Long, Broad and Sharpsight, they set off in search of more adventures.

They may even be adventuring still.

The Snow Queen

Once, on a little street in a big town, lived two friends named Gerda and Kay. All summer long, they played together happily in the sunshine.

Then winter came, and it was too cold to play outside. Instead, they sat by the stove while Kay's grandmother told them stories. One day, she told them about the Snow Queen.

"On days like this, you must watch out for the Snow Queen," she said. "She's a cold, dangerous woman! She lives in the icy north, but in winter she flies around and peers through windows, frosting up the glass. But she can't come inside, it's too warm – and she can't abide a warm heart. If you are warm and loving, you will always see her for what she is."

161

That night, Kay glanced out of his window.

A few snowflakes were still falling. One flake grew bigger and bigger, until it turned into a beautiful woman made of shining, glittering ice and robed in starry snow.

"The Snow Queen," breathed Kay.

She looked at Kay and beckoned. Frightened, he stumbled back. When he looked up, she was gone.

By spring, Kay had forgotten all about the Snow Queen. He played happily with Gerda and helped her tend her window box full of roses.

One day, as they watered the roses, Kay clutched his eye and his chest. "Ouch!"

"What's the matter?" asked Gerda at once.

"Something stabbed me," moaned Kay.

Gerda looked. "I can't see anything," she said. But although she couldn't see them, a tiny splinter of ice had stabbed Kay's eye, and another had pierced his heart...

At once, Kay's heart began to freeze and he started to change. "Leave me alone," he snapped at Gerda.

"Kay, what's wrong?" she cried.

"I'm fine. *You're* the problem. You and your worm-eaten roses!" He tore up the flowers, making Gerda sob. Kay laughed and ran away.

Now Kay and Gerda didn't play together any more. Kay just wanted to argue and make fun of people in the street. He told his grandmother her stories were boring. He told Gerda she was ugly and stupid. Gerda still loved him, but there was nothing she could do.

When winter came, Kay ignored Gerda and went to play with the other boys in the town square. As he reached the square, a dazzling white sleigh drove up.

"Come and sit with me," said the driver.

Smiling, Kay obeyed. His frozen heart had blinded him to danger, for it was none other than the Snow Queen. She draped a snowy white rug over him, and Kay felt as if he was sinking into a snowdrift. Then she gave him an icy kiss, and Kay forgot the cold. She kissed him again, and he forgot home, and Gerda, and everything else.

The sleigh flew out of town, taking Kay with it. The snow whirled thick and fast, and the wind whistled and roared. They flew over woods and lakes, land and sea, with only the light of the moon to show them the way.

Back home, no one knew where Kay had gone. His grandmother wept, thinking he must have drowned, and Gerda cried too. But when spring came, she began to wonder.

"Is he really dead?" she asked the swallows.

"We don't believe it," they chirped in reply. "Why not ask the river? It flows a long way, it may have seen him."

So Gerda put on her best red shoes and set off.

At the river, she took off her shoes. "Dear river, I will give you my shoes if you will help me find Kay." She threw them into the water, but the waves washed them back again.

"Maybe I didn't throw them far enough," she thought. She climbed into a boat to try again – but it wasn't tied up properly and she was swept away.

"Perhaps the river is taking me to Kay," she thought.

She floated along for hours. Eventually, the boat began to drift ashore. On the bank stood a pretty cottage, surrounded by rose bushes and cherry trees. An old woman hobbled over.

"I'm looking for Kay, have you seen him?" said Gerda.

"No, but come and have some cherries, and tell me about him," said the woman.

The woman wasn't wicked, but she was lonely and she longed for a daughter. She knew a little magic and so she cast a spell to make Gerda forget her old life. She even magicked away the rose bushes, in case they reminded Gerda of the window box.

The spell worked. Gerda's memories became a distant dream. She spent days playing in the woman's flower garden, and nights sleeping under a soft, flowery quilt.

She might have stayed forever, but one day, she found a hat painted with flowers. One of them looked familiar...

"A rose!" All at once, her memories came flooding back. "Kay! How could I forget? I've wasted so much time."

Gerda hurried off without even saying goodbye.

Outside the woman's garden, summer was over.
Everything seemed cold and bleak, and she was nearly
in despair when she heard a crow calling.

"*Caw, caw.* Good *caw* day."

"Have you seen Kay?" Gerda asked.

"Is Kay a boy?" said the crow. "Then yes, maybe.
There is a boy who married a Princess. He was a poor boy,
with creaky boots, but the Princess fell in love with him."

"That must be Kay," said Gerda excitedly. "His boots creak
and he is very handsome. Can you take me to him?"

So that night, the crow helped her creep into the Princess's
palace. It led her through dark doorways and halls filled with
flickering shadows, into a room where two silken lilies hung from
a golden stem. In one slept a Princess, and in the other...

"Oh!" exclaimed Gerda sadly. "He isn't Kay."

The noise woke the Prince and Princess. They were startled to
see Gerda, but she looked so small and sad that they immediately
took pity on her. "What's the matter?" they asked.

Gerda told them about her quest.

"Let us help you," said the Princess. She gave Gerda a warm
coat and new boots.

Then the Prince helped Gerda into a golden carriage, loaded with cakes and gingerbread, and waved her on her way.

The carriage was rolling through a dark forest when a band of robbers rushed out, lured by its golden gleam. They seized the horses and gobbled up the cakes. Then they turned to Gerda.

"She looks sweet," cackled an old robber woman. "Perhaps we should eat her too!"

"No," said a little robber girl. "I want her. She can be my friend." And she took Gerda home to meet her pets – two tame wood pigeons and a reindeer called Ba.

"Why were you in the forest?" asked the robber girl.

"I was looking for Kay," Gerda replied.

The pigeons rustled their feathers. "Kay, Kay," they cooed. "The Snow Queen has him. We saw him in her sleigh, flying over our forest."

"Where would she take him?" pleaded Gerda.

Ba the reindeer tossed his antlers. "To her castle in the far north," he grunted.

"Do you know the way?" asked the robber girl.

"Of course," snorted Ba. "I was born in the north."

"Then you must carry Gerda there," said the robber girl.

167

She gave Gerda a loaf and ham, and helped her climb onto Ba's back. "Now, run!" she told Ba. "And take care of Gerda."

"Farewell," called Gerda, as Ba leaped away.

As they journeyed north, the land grew colder.

Soon, Ba was running over snow and ice, and the bread and ham were all gone. Gerda was very cold and hungry by the time Ba stopped outside a little sloping hut.

An old woman came out to greet them. Gerda was so cold she could hardly speak, but Ba told her story for her.

"You poor child," said the woman. "You still have far to go. Come in and warm yourself, and I will give you a note to take to my friend. She is wise and may be able to help you."

The woman scribbled while Gerda sipped hot soup. Then they set off again, galloping over snowy plains while the northern lights lit up the sky in blue flashes.

At daybreak, they arrived at a second hut. Another old woman appeared to welcome them.

Gerda gave her the note. The woman read it carefully and listened to Gerda's tale before consulting an old manuscript.

"The Snow Queen has enchanted Kay," she muttered. "To set him free, Gerda must remove the splinters of ice from his eye and heart."

"Can you help her?" pleaded Ba.

The woman lowered her voice, so Gerda could not hear. "I can give her no greater power than she has already. See how far she has come, with only her warm heart to guide her! Just take her to the edge of the Snow Queen's garden. She must do the rest by herself."

So Ba carried Gerda once more, to the edge of the Snow Queen's garden – and there he left her, alone in the falling snow.

Gerda shivered and started to walk. With each step, the snow grew thicker, until she was surrounded by a whirling blizzard. Monstrous creatures formed out of the snowflakes – spiky porcupines, twisting snakes and bristling bears. They were the Snow Queen's guards.

Gerda was terrified, but she didn't run away.

Instead, she mouthed the words of a prayer. It was so cold,
she could see her breath like steam. The steam billowed
up around her and took on the shape of angels.
Gerda suddenly felt warmer.
The angels attacked the snow monsters,
making them shatter into broken flakes. Gerda ran on,
unhindered, into the Snow Queen's castle.

She found herself in a vast, glittering hall, carved from windblown snow. Ahead lay a frozen lake and, in the middle of the lake, an empty throne – for the Snow Queen was away from home, conjuring snowstorms in warmer lands.

A small figure was hunched at the base of the throne. It was Kay, blue with cold and puzzling over a pile of ice.

Each piece of ice bore a letter. "If you can discover what they spell," the Snow Queen had said before she left, "you can have whatever you like – a new pair of skates, the whole world... even your freedom," she had added, laughing.

Kay wanted to solve the puzzle, but his brain was numb with cold. So he sat staring helplessly at the letters – and that was how Gerda found him.

"Kay!" Gerda ran up and flung her arms around him, but he didn't move. "Oh Kay," she wept. "Don't you remember me, and home, and our roses?"

Hot tears splashed onto Kay's chest, thawing his heart and washing away the splinter of ice lodged there. Slowly, he looked up. "Gerda?" he said wonderingly.

She nodded, and Kay wept too. His tears washed away the splinter of ice in his eye and he was his old self again.

He jumped up and hugged her, and laughed so loudly that even the pieces of ice danced around. When the pieces fell back into place, they spelled out the word Kay had been searching for... "Eternity," he cried, pointing. "I'm free!"

Kay and Gerda left the ice castle hand-in-hand. At the edge of the garden, Ba was waiting with another reindeer to carry them home.

It was a long journey, and longer because they stopped to thank everyone who had helped Gerda along the way.

As they went on, they saw signs of spring – green shoots and early flowers – and by the time they reached their little street, it was summer. The window box was blooming with roses and Kay's grandmother was waiting to welcome them.

"We did it," they said. "The Snow Queen tried to steal Kay, but we defeated her."

"This truly is a happy ending," she answered – and behind her, the roses in the window box nodded their heads in agreement.

THE RAVEN AND THE RING

Long ago, a terrible dragon came crawling out of the north. It had stony scales and spiky teeth, and wherever it went, it breathed fire and destruction. The King's soldiers did their best to fight it, but their spears and swords and arrows simply shattered against the dragon's hard, stone sides.

Then the King sent for his magician.

"You are old and wise," said the King. "Tell me, do you know a way to defeat the dragon?"

"Ordinary magic is no use," said the magician, frowning. "Such a monster can only be destroyed using King Solomon's ring. The ring gives the wearer great power. There's just one problem – the ring was lost years ago."

175

A young soldier named Mattias had been listening closely. "I'll look for it!" he offered. The King's daughter cast him an admiring glance, and he blushed.

The King looked into the boy's brave face and nodded. "Very well. But you will have to go alone – I can't spare any more men."

"Take this," said the magician, handing Mattias a shining flask. "It is a potion of herbs and moonlight. Drink it, and you will be able to understand the language of birds. They fly far and wide, and see much. They may be able to help you."

So Mattias drank the potion and set off. He was all alone, but he didn't feel lonely – for wherever he went, there were birds. He listened as chirpy robins argued over juicy worms, and swallows sang of the lands beyond the sea.

But nowhere did he hear of the missing ring – until one day, as he rested by a spring, he noticed two ravens flapping around in a tree.

"What an ugly fellow," croaked one, turning its head to stare at Mattias. "He's not like the moon-witch."

"Indeed, she is very beautiful," cawed the other, older bird. "And so powerful, you'd think she had King Solomon's ring."

"*Aha,*" thought Mattias.

"The boy clearly doesn't know this spring belongs to her," the old raven continued. "She'll be here as soon as the moon rises, and she won't like finding a stranger here."

Curious, Mattias hid behind a bush and waited. Sure enough, as the moon rose and touched the surface of the water with silver, the witch appeared...

Mattias caught his breath. She was very beautiful, just as the ravens had said; but there was something hard and cold about her face.

She stooped and dipped her hands in the water.

Mattias leaned forward, and a leaf rustled. The witch spun around. "Who's there?" she snapped.

"This is *my* spring," she went on crossly, as Mattias stepped into the open. "I should turn you into a frog for trespassing! Tell me – who are you and why are you here?"

"I am sorry to disturb you, my lady," Mattias said, with a bow. "I was tired and I stopped to rest." He was careful not to mention any ring.

The witch nodded, pleased with his handsome face and polite manner. "In that case, I forgive you. But my palace is a much better place to rest. Come!" She held out her hand.

In the tree above, the old raven let out an urgent caw. "Whatever you do, don't kiss her, or you will never leave!"

Mattias nodded gratefully at the bird, and went.

The witch led Mattias to a beautiful garden, full of night-blooming flowers. In the middle stood a splendid palace of white marble.

After offering the young soldier food and drink, the witch began to show off her riches. She threw open heavy wooden chests, revealing great heaps of silver, pearls and moonstones, glimmering and shimmering in the cold, moonlit hall. Mattias was amazed; he didn't know they were all an illusion created by magic.

"Now," said the witch proudly, "I will show you the greatest treasure of all." And pulling out a key, she unlocked the last chest. For a moment, Mattias thought it was empty – but then, lying at the very bottom, he saw a little brass ring.

The witch held up the ring. "This is my most prized possession," she told Mattias. "But I will give it to you in exchange for a kiss."

Mattias remembered the raven's warning and shuddered, but did his best to hide it. "What's so special about this ring?"

"It used to belong to King Solomon," said the witch proudly. "It gives the wearer magical powers. With it, you may fly like a bird and become invisible at will, have the strength of a hundred men and be protected from all harm."

"Impossible!" claimed Mattias, laughing.

"I'll show you," said the witch. She slipped on the ring and rose into the air, her long hair rippling behind her.

"Very impressive," said Mattias. "But how do I know it will work for me?"

"Try it," said the witch, holding out the ring.

Mattias put it on. Then he sprang up – and found himself hovering in mid-air. "Whoopee!"

He tapped a stone in the wall beside him, and it shattered into pieces.

"Now for my kiss," said the witch, reaching out her arms with a chilling smile.

Instead of answering, Mattias vanished. Silent and invisible, he flew through the hole in the wall and away.

"Come back here," called the witch, furiously grabbing at the air. But she was too late. Mattias was off to seek the dragon, leaving her far behind.

From the air, Mattias could see for miles. Dawn was breaking, and tiny clouds of smoke were starting to rise from the villages and farms. On the horizon, one smoke cloud was bigger and blacker than all the others.

"The dragon!"

As he drew closer, he saw burned-out houses and blackened fields. Then, curled up in a nest of charred stones, he spotted the dragon itself. There were no other living creatures in sight, for the dragon had eaten them all.

Even with the ring, Mattias knew he needed a weapon. He looked around and saw a giant spear abandoned by the King's soldiers. "Just the thing," he thought, landing beside it.

He heard fluttering wings, and looked up. It was the wise old raven. "I'm glad you got away from the witch," it croaked. "Now I see you mean to fight the dragon."

Mattias nodded. "Have you got any advice for me?"

The raven looked thoughtful. "The dragon is drowsy from eating, but you must be careful how you approach it. Be slow, silent and invisible! If it sees or hears you, it will try to gobble you up. Only show yourself when you are within striking distance.

Then it will open its mouth to eat you – and you can cast the spear between its teeth."

Mattias nodded. "That is good advice," he said.

"Thank you." He stooped to grasp the spear – and gasped.

It was huge and heavy, designed to be handled by many men. Even with the magic from the ring, he could only just lift it.

Making himself invisible, he inched forwards. His arms ached and sweat dripped down his face. When he was within a spear's distance, he stopped and swallowed hard.

"It's now or never," he told himself firmly. And with that, he made himself visible again. "Dinner time!" he announced to the startled dragon.

Snorting angry sparks, the monster opened its jaws.

"That's right..." With all his might, Mattias hurled the spear straight at it.

The dragon roared like thunder. Its tail beat the ground and it bellowed forth flames. Without the ring, Mattias would have been killed. But instead, when the smoke cleared, it was the dragon which lay lifeless on ground. Mattias was completely unharmed.

"I did it," he sighed. "Thanks to the raven and the ring."

The dragon's death brought great rejoicing. Mattias was hailed as a hero, and married the King's daughter; and the old raven was awarded a royal medal. With the help of the magical ring, the King's lands prospered. And no dragon ever dared to trouble them again.

The Emperor and the Wise Man

Long ago, in India, there was an Emperor who loved playing games. In fact, he spent so much time playing games that he never left his palace. So he never saw how many of his people went hungry, while the palace storerooms overflowed with rice.

One day, a wise man came to the palace, carrying a magnificent chessboard. "Will you play chess with me, Majesty?" he asked. "If you win, I will give you my board and tell everyone how clever you are."

The Emperor looked admiringly at the board. Its squares were made of glowing black ebony and gleaming white mother-of-pearl. "And if you win?" he asked.

185

"All I want is some rice, enough to cover the board in this way – one grain on the first square, two grains on the second square, four grains on the third, eight grains on the fourth..."

"Stop," cried the Emperor. "I get it. Double each time?"

"Yes," said the wise man. "Double on each square, until the end of the board."

The Emperor counted the squares; there were eight rows of eight, making sixty-four in total. "That's not much of a prize," he laughed. "Why don't you ask for something else?"

"The rice will be plenty," said the wise man.

"Very well, I agree," said the Emperor. "If you play as badly as you bargain," he added quietly, "I'll win easily."

The game started. The Emperor played well – but the wise man played better. Soon, the Emperor was frowning. He thought long and hard about every move, but it was no good. One by one, the wise man took his pieces, until there was no doubt who had won.

"Check-mate," said the wise man.

The Emperor sighed, and snapped his fingers. "Bring the rice!" Servants came running and began counting grains onto squares. "One, two, four, eight, sixteen..."

The Emperor watched, smiling. "Now don't you wish you'd asked for something else?"

"No," said the wise man. "This is all I want, and more."

The servants kept counting. "Thirty-two, sixty-four, one hundred and twenty-eight..."

That was the end of the first row. They paused. "We can't fit the grains on the squares."

"Use bowls then," ordered the Emperor. "Hurry up!"

The counting continued. "Two hundred and fifty-six, five hundred and twelve, one thousand and twenty-four, two thousand and forty-eight..."

The rice was mounding up faster and faster. Now, the servants were counting in great, slithering handfuls. The bowls overflowed, so they heaped it on the floor.

Before the end of the fourth row, they were counting in sackfuls. A few squares later, it was cartloads – and the numbers were still doubling...

Soon, rice was piled right up to the ceiling and the servants were looking worried. "Majesty," they whispered. "All of the storerooms are empty."

"I must pay my debts," snapped the Emperor. "How much rice is there in the country?"

"About a million tons, your Majesty."

But halfway along the sixth row, it was all promised to the wise man – and they were far from the end of the board...

The Emperor shook his head slowly. "I have made a mistake," he said gruffly. "This is a debt I cannot pay."

"I know," said the wise man, gently. "All the rice in all the world would not be enough to reach the last square. But I will consider the debt paid, if you share what you do have, and feed everyone who comes to the palace hungry."

The Emperor nodded. "I will," he said. "And I would like you to be my first guest."

So, that evening, the wise man brought all the hungry people to the palace.

The Emperor hung his head to see how many there were. "I'm sorry," he said. "You won't go hungry again."

And he invited them all inside for a delicious feast of spicy curries and tangy pickles, with bowl after bowl of hot, buttery rice.

About the Stories

People have been telling magical stories for thousands of years, although they only began to write them down and call them *fairytales* about four hundred years ago. Popular tales were told and retold, changing a little each time, so you can find many different versions of them today.

This treasury includes some of the best-known tales from Europe and around the world.

★ *The Frog Prince, The Fairy at the Well, Twelve Dancing Princesses, Fearless Hans* – these are all based on traditional tales, first written down in Germany about two hundred years ago, by the Brothers Grimm.

★ *Cinderella, Sleeping Beauty* – these stories are partly based on tales from France, as told about three hundred years ago by Charles Perrault, and partly on versions by the Brothers Grimm; but the oldest version of Cinderella comes from Ancient Egypt.

★ *The Magic Tinderbox, The Snow Queen* – these stories were written nearly two hundred years ago, by Danish author Hans Christian Andersen, who was in turn inspired by tales from his childhood.

★ *Beauty and the Beast* – this was written over two hundred and fifty years ago in France, by Madame de Villeneuve and Madame de Beaumont.

★ *The Magician's Horse* – this tale comes from a collection of stories from the Middle East, known as *The Arabian Nights*.

★ *The Bluebird* – this is based on an old Spanish tale.

★ *Puss in Boots* – this story is partly based on a version by Charles Perrault, and partly on an Italian folktale.

★ *Prince Ivan and the Firebird* – this is a traditional tale from Russia.

★ *The Emperor and the Wise Man* – this story is based on an old Indian legend.

★ *East of the Sun, West of the Moon* – this comes from Scandinavia.

★ *Long, Broad and Sharpsight* – this is a version of a traditional story from central Europe.

★ *The Youngest Princess* – this is an old story from western Europe; the same story inspired William Shakespeare, when he wrote his play *King Lear*.

★ *The Raven and the Ring* – this is based on a traditional tale from northern Europe.

Designed by Nicola Butler and Jessica Johnson
Additional artwork by Abigail Brown
Edited by Lesley Sims and Jenny Tyler
Digital manipulation by Nick Wakeford

First published in 2009 by Usborne Publishing Ltd,
83-85 Saffron Hill, London, EC1N 8RT, England.
WWW.USBORNE.COM